More Short & Shivery

MORE SHORT & SHIVERY

THIRTY TERRIFYING TALES

RETOLD BY ROBERT D. SAN SOUCI

Illustrated by Katherine Coville and Jacqueline Rogers

Delacorte  Press

Published by
Delacorte Press
Bantam Doubleday Dell Publishing Group, Inc.
1540 Broadway
New York, New York 10036

Library of Congress Cataloging in Publication Data

San Souci, Robert D.
    More short & shivery: thirty terrifying tales/retold by Robert D. San
Souci; illustrated by Katherine Coville and Jacqueline Rogers.
        p.   cm.
    Summary: A collection of scary folktales from the United States,
China, England, Italy, Russia, and other countries around the world.
    ISBN 0-385-32102-3
    1. Tales. 2. Ghost stories. [1. Folklore. 2. Ghosts—Folklore.
3. Supernatural—Folklore.] I. Coville, Katherine, ill. II. Rogers,
Jacqueline, ill. III. Title. IV. Title: More short and shivery.
PZ8.1.S227Mo 1994
[398.25]—dc20   94-479   CIP   AC

Manufactured in the United States of America

September 1994

10 9 8 7 6 5 4 3 2 1

Contents

Introduction

Welcome, old friends and new, to this second collection of some of my favorite scary tales, retold from the ghostlore of many different peoples and places. Since the first volume of *Short & Shivery* was published, I've had a chance to visit with young readers all around the country who have helped me decide what stories to include here. I am thankful to these friends in Alabama, California, Colorado, Delaware, Illinois, Kansas, Massachusetts, Michigan, Nebraska, Ohio, Oklahoma, Oregon, Washington, and elsewhere—this book is dedicated to all of you.

I hope you enjoy this book as much as the first *Short & Shivery*. One of the nice things about the present volume is that it lets me share stories there wasn't room for in my earlier book. I've also made an effort to include stories from parts of the world not covered in the first book. In the pages that follow are ghostly tales from Brazil, China, Haiti, Italy, Mexico, Nigeria, Papua New Guinea, Scotland, and Spain—as well as many parts of the United States.

You'll meet Bishop Hatto, who *really* had a problem with mice . . . Jubal Lescot, who learns why children shouldn't go poking around cemeteries at midnight . . . Tom Walker, who should have read the not-so-fine print in his contract with the Devil . . . and poor Georgette, who finds a bundle that should *not* be unwrapped until Christmas—or *ever*!

Here are such bone-chilling creatures as the duppy, the yara, the draug, and the windigo who haunt lonely houses, forests, rivers, and seashores all over the world. You'll also run into a helpful skeleton, a rolling head, a golden arm, and some witches' eyes—all of which refuse to rest in peace (or pieces).

For those who want to learn more about these stories and where they came from, I have included a section of "Notes on Sources" at the end of this book.

So settle back, relax—no, on second thought, don't plan on getting too relaxed! Truth in advertising means that I have to warn you that these are *not* warm-and-fuzzy stories. They have proven popular—often for centuries—precisely because they have provided readers and listeners plenty of thrills and chills. They are guaranteed to raise a healthy crop of Halloween-style goose bumps in *any* season.

In short, the stories in this book have teeth. Sharp ones. But then, isn't that what you're looking for? It must be, since you're reading these words right now. Well, you've been warned: "Reader, beware!" Proceed at your own risk.

"Hold Him, Tabb!"

(United States—Virginia)

Before the railroads were built in Virginia, supplies had to be carried from one town to another on wagons. One afternoon, late in December, a number of supply wagons traveling together were caught in a sudden snowstorm.

The drivers pushed on through the freezing cold and heavy snow until they came to an abandoned farm very near the road.

"Looks like a good place to sit out the storm," said a man named Tabb.

"I heard that the house is haunted," said another driver, heading toward the barn. "I'm going to bed down in one of the stalls with the horses."

Several other drivers said they had heard some pretty bad things about the house, too; one man said he'd heard that, for almost twenty-five years, not a single person who had stayed overnight remained alive to see the dawn. Most of the men decided they preferred to sleep in the barn with the animals.

"Well," said Tabb, who was braver than the rest, "I'm not afraid of any haunts. And I'm not about to sleep with horses and cowards when there's a real house just up the hill."

When he'd finished unhooking his horses, Tabb marched up to the house, which looked forlorn and run-down but not in the least daunting.

Inside he found a big potbellied stove and a healthy supply of wood. He built a cheery fire, cooked and ate his supper, and finally bedded down on a couch he dragged near the stove. He slept peacefully through the night, without being disturbed by anything except an odd bit of wood snapping inside the stove.

Just before sunrise he woke up, stretched, and said, "What a bunch of fools those other fellows are to have stayed down with the horses, when they could have stayed in here, just as warm and comfortable as me!"

No sooner had he finished speaking than he heard a rumbling laugh overhead.

Looking up to the ceiling, he saw a large man dressed in white clothes stretched out under the rafters, as though he were sticking to them.

Before Tabb could make a move, the man in white dropped right down on top of him. They started tussling, rolling back and forth across the floor, knocking the furniture in the room every which way. The two made so much noise that the men in the barn heard it and ran up the hill to see what was the matter.

Not daring to set foot in the house, they all clustered at the windows, prying open the shutters and leaning in. They saw the struggle going on. Tabb and the man in white seemed about equally matched: One minute, Tabb would be on top; the next, the man in white.

One of the drivers cried, "Hold him, Tabb! Hold him!"

"You can bet your soul I will!" yelled Tabb. "I've got him for sure!"

A minute later, the two fighters came crashing through a window, sending the drivers scattering.

"Hold him, Tabb! Hold him!" another driver shouted.

"You can bet your life I will!" cried Tabb. "I've got him right where I want him!"

The next moment, the man in white began whirling Tabb around and flung him onto the roof of the house. Then the stranger jumped up after him, so the drivers had to stand some distance away just to see what was happening.

"Hold him, Tabb! Hold him!" they yelled, one after another.

"You can just bet your boots I will!" said Tabb, panting. "He won't get away from me!"

Now the two wrestlers on the roof were so knotted together that the drivers down below had a hard time telling which arm or leg belonged to which. Then, as the drivers watched open-mouthed, the fighters began floating up off the roof.

One of the drivers cupped his hands around his mouth and bellowed, "Hold him, Tabb! Hold him!"

"I got him; and he's got me, too!" shouted Tabb.

Then the man in white carried Tabb straight up into the air until they were both out of sight.

And nothing was ever seen of Tabb after that.

The Witches' Eyes

(Spanish American—American Southwest)

Many years ago there was an elderly widower named Don Pedro who eased his loneliness by spending one or two evenings each week visiting two sisters—themselves his own age or nearly so—who lived across the road from his house. Though his other neighbors warned him in harsh whispers that the women were *brujas*—witches—the old man ignored these taletellers. He sipped chocolate with cinnamon, played a card game called *canoncito*, or shared *cuentos*—stories—of the old days with his friends Doña Inez and Doña Teresa.

Don Pedro knew that one sister was several years older than the other, but he was never certain which was the elder—and he was too polite to ask. The two dressed alike in skirts of stiff black material and carried identical fans of ebony silk. They might have been twins—save that one had eyes the deep color of coffee flecked with gold, while the other had paler, tea-colored eyes, likewise gold-flecked.

Always, just before midnight, the women would lay down their cards or stop their storytelling and murmur, "Pedro, you must go home now."

Though he would beg to play just one more hand or hear a story to its end, they would shake their heads firmly and say, "You must go *now*."

When he mentioned this to his neighbors, they said, "*Sí,*

sí, this proves they are witches. They must be rid of you to begin their night's mischief."

"Do you suppose they go flying about under the moon?" asked Pedro, laughing at the thought.

His neighbors would grow red in the face at his laughter, and shrug their shoulders.

But Don Pedro found that the suspicions of his friends were feeding his own curiosity. Often, when he was unable to sleep, he would sit at a window and watch the silent *casa* —house—across the road. But the only thing out of the ordinary he noticed were the comings and goings of two lean cats, one with dark brown fur and one with tawny fur, that prowled the women's moonlit garden. One night they seemed to sense that he was spying on them, for they arched their backs and hissed in his direction. This disturbed Pedro so that he returned to his bed, though sleep did not come to him until dawn's light streaked the sky.

The next morning he decided to take a little gift of *pan dulce,* a sweet bread, across the road to his neighbors. He noticed that both women had dark circles under their eyes.

"Buenos días. I chanced to be up last night and saw two cats near your door," he said. "Are they pets?"

"There are no cats here!" said the sister with coffee-colored eyes.

"You must have been dreaming, Pedro," added the other sister. Her tea-colored eyes glittered with a harshness the old man had never seen before.

"No doubt I was mistaken," said Don Pedro, and he handed over his gift with a hasty *"Adiós."*

·   ·   ·

There was a further mystery. Sometimes while the three talked and played cards in the evening, one or the other sister would mention something that had happened in a distant town. Days later, Don Pedro would learn that they had spoken the truth. But how could they know so quickly about something that had happened a day's journey away?

When he questioned them, they merely laughed and said that they had heard the news in the market square.

Then, one night, Pedro was awakened by the sound of a cat howling. Staring at the darkened *casa* across the way, he clearly saw two cats scurry from the stoop and around the corner of the house.

Determined to find answers to his questions, Don Pedro marched across the road and knocked loudly on the door of the sisters' dwelling. The place remained silent, the whitewashed adobe gleaming under the midnight moon. He knocked several times, yet neither woman came in answer.

Afraid for his friends' well-being, he tried the door. It was unlocked, and he pushed it open.

"Doña Inez, Doña Teresa," he called, "are you well?"

Inside, the rooms were empty. The only light came from moonlight streaming through the lattices and the faint glow of embers in the corner chimney. In the red light of the coals, Don Pedro saw to his horror that two sets of eyes—like the glass eyes from a china doll—sat on a dish on a stool in front of the hearth. One pair of eyes were deep brown; one pair, tawny; both were flecked with gold.

"Oh!" cried Don Pedro, blessing himself. In his haste to escape, he stumbled and lost his balance. His foot shot out and knocked the stool over. The dish tumbled into the fire. Instantly there was a puff of brown and a puff of tan smoke that flew up the chimney. The frantic man used a poker to search the coals and ashes. But though he rescued the dish, not a trace remained of its awful contents.

Frightened, Don Pedro hurried home. A little later he heard two cats begin a terrible howling. He did not need to look to guess that it was coming from inside the house across the road.

The next day, Don Pedro did not know what to do. It was his regular evening for calling on the sisters. He was afraid to face them—but he was more afraid that if he didn't, they would suspect him of being the one who had made such mischief the night before. At last he decided to bluff his way through a visit.

He dressed especially well, and took two roses from his small garden. Then, with a trembling hand, he knocked on the door—remembering all too well how that door had opened onto a frightful scene only a few hours before.

"*¡Pase usted!*" called Doña Inez, and her sister also invited him, "Come in!"

As he entered, he noticed that the lattices were still shut. The room was dark. No lamps had been lit, and the fireplace was cold. The two women murmured polite words but kept their faces turned away or hidden by their black silk fans. When they moved, they seemed clumsy, as though even the dim light bothered their eyes.

"Alas, Don Pedro," said Doña Inez in a sad voice, her face averted so that she was gazing at the cold hearth, "I am afraid that we will no longer be able to share our evenings with you."

"Yes," said her sister, sighing behind her fan, "we have other duties that must occupy our time from now on."

"I see, of course," said Don Pedro, who only wanted to

be away from the house. His nervousness had gotten the best of him. As he fumbled for the door, he was aware that Doña Inez had turned to gaze at him suspiciously, while Doña Teresa had momentarily lowered her fan.

At that moment, he pulled open the door. The sudden light revealed the sisters staring at him with the round eyes of cats. "Go! Close the door!" they hissed, turning away in pain.

Don Pedro quickly drew the door shut and fled.

That night and every night thereafter he locked his doors and windows at evening, and did not unlock them until the sun was high above the eastern mountains. And he slept with his rosary clutched tightly in his hand.

Sometimes he thought he heard the sounds of cats' paws at his door or window. But he prayed a "Hail Mary" aloud, and the sound went away.

Shortly thereafter, his strange neighbors departed in a carriage hung with black velvet curtains. They never returned, and the house remained empty for as long as Don Pedro lived.

The Duppy

(Haiti)

Jubal Lescot was only six when his Aunt Albertine died. The old woman had been sharp-tongued, and quick to accuse the child of misdeeds—more often imagined than real. So the boy was more relieved than sorry. He was glad not to have her scolding him all the time, calling him "lazy" and "good-fo'-not'in'."

Albertine Lescot was buried in a small churchyard on a hillside near the shanty where she had lived with her brother and his family. Through the banana trees, mimboms, and palm fronds that grew all around the cemetery, the mourners now and then got a glimpse of the distant roofs of Port-au-Prince, the capital of Haiti.

Before the funeral, Jubal overheard several of the neighbors saying that a duppy—a kind of ghost—was sure to rise from the old woman's grave at cock crow on the third night after her burial.

"What's dat duppy?" he asked his mother.

"Somet'in' you don' never want t' meet up wit'," she told him. "Somet'in' dat can take hold o' you if you not careful—or if you don' believe."

"It a ghost, but not a ghost," his father said. "Everyone have evil in him; but when he alive, his brain and his heart control dat evil. After de spirit go away, dat evil part be lef' behin'. If it don' have nothin' t' keep it from doin' whatever it want, it go out into de worl', where it do terrible t'ings."

"So we get a magic man t' put a spell on dat duppy an' keep it stayin' in de grave," his mother explained. "It a bad t'ing to let a duppy stay 'mong Christian folk." Then she shook her finger at Jubal. "Any child dat ain' a foolish child will keep in his bed wit' de shutters close', 'til magic make dat duppy res' quiet fo' all time," she warned him.

Because he was a curious boy, Jubal quietly got out of bed on the third night after Albertine's funeral. While his parents slept in their little bedroom behind a heavy blanket that served as a door, Jubal stepped out into the warm night.

In the moonlight—so bright it almost felt hot—the boy had no trouble picking out the trail that led from the shanty to the neighborhood cemetery. There he found he wasn't quite brave enough to set foot inside the graveyard. So he climbed a huge mango tree that overhung the rusty iron fence surrounding the burial ground. From here he had a clear view of his aunt's grave, halfway up the slope.

He perched where several massive branches joined, to watch. But as time slipped by and the night grew darker around him, Jubal remembered the warnings his parents had given him. He began to think he would be better off back in his bed. He was already risking a scolding and a spanking for leaving the house after dark. Now he began to be afraid of what else he might be risking, alone in the dark, spying on ghosts.

No! he told himself, *I come dis far, I ain' gonna give up now.* So he clung stubbornly to his perch as the night yawned toward morning. He dozed a little, unaware for the most part that he had slept at all.

Then, in the last hours before sunup, Jubal saw a huge bubble of white light squeeze out of the mounded earth of his aunt's grave. It made a wet, popping sound as it floated free of the ground.

The moon had set, but it seemed to Jubal that the earth

had given birth to a second moon. Inside the man-sized globe of light swam a lazy swirl of shadow, like a just-forming chicken in an egg held up to a candle. It was lit by an unhealthy glow that seemed to seep out, rather than shine, from inside. The surface had a damp look to it.

For a moment the slimy bubble hovered just above the grave. Then, as if it sensed the boy in hiding, it began to move toward the mango tree. The lower half of the bubble slid right through the stone and metal grave markers that dotted the hillside.

Jubal knew that it was coming for him. He scrambled down from the tree and began running through the thick jungle toward home. With only starlight to help him pick out the thread of the path, he stumbled often over roots and rocks. He did not dare look back, because he knew he would see the terrifying bubble of white light stained with shadows following him, getting closer.

Light from behind made the path ahead easier to see; he knew that meant the deadly glowing thing had almost caught up with him. When he rounded a bend in the trail and saw that he was near home, Jubal began to scream for help.

Then, trying to force his aching legs to go faster, he tripped. He tumbled forward into a puddle that soaked his clothes and filled his nose with a rotten smell.

He heard a sound like a rushing wind coming down the path behind him, followed by another sound, as though a great fire was sizzling and crisping the leaves on the trees.

Too scared to move, Jubal buried his face in his arms and waited for the duppy to touch him, to burn him to ashes.

Something grabbed him roughly by his shirt collar and jerked him, screeching like a crazy gull, to his feet. He windmilled his arms, keeping his eyes tightly shut.

He felt himself shaken fiercely by the shoulders while

his father shouted, "Open yo' eyes, boy! And shut yo' mout'! What givin' you such fits?"

Carefully, Jubal opened his eyes and looked around the starlit glade. They were alone; the forest was silent and dark. "Tell me what you be doin' here," his father said angrily, his strong hands never loosening their grip on Jubal's shoulders.

"A duppy, Papa," Jubal said when he could catch his breath. "It be tryin' t' touch me and kill me!"

"Why it be chasin' you?"

"At de graveyard—" Jubal began.

But his father interrupted him. "You been spyin' on dat duppy? Don' you know dat vexes him?" He looked nervously around the clearing. "Get 'long home, quick as you can. In de mornin', you gotta fetch de priest t' lay dat duppy t' rest."

As they hurried along, with many glances back over their shoulders, Jubal's father said, "I should whip you so's you never forget what you done tonight. An' so's you won' do it no more. But I can see by yo' face dat you won' go vexin' no duppy ever again."

And Jubal, seeing their cabin ahead, with his mother standing anxiously in the doorway, felt he was the luckiest boy alive—just to *be* alive.

Two Snakes

(China)

In ancient China, there was once a man who decided to hunt on a certain mountain people said was the home of many strange creatures. But the hunter paid no attention to these old stories. He climbed high up the wooded slopes in search of game. Though he often heard the calls of birds and the sounds of animals in the thickets, and though he kept his bow and arrow at the ready, he did not catch sight of a single pheasant or deer.

At night, discouraged, he built a rude shelter of branches, telling himself that the next day would bring him the bounty that had so far eluded him.

As he huddled in his cloak, trying to fall asleep, he was startled to hear the sound of a heavy footfall in the clearing outside. Peering out of his lean-to, he saw a tall, thin figure dressed in white robes. The man, who was more than ten feet tall, spoke in a thin, piping voice.

"I have come to ask your help," the stranger said. "I am going to fight against my enemy tomorrow. Help me, and you will be abundantly rewarded."

The hunter was delighted. "I am more than willing to help," he said. "What must I do?"

"Tomorrow at mealtime, go to the stream that flows to the east of here," the visitor said. "My enemy will be coming from the north, and I shall be meeting him from the south. Remember that I shall be the one in white, and he will be the one in yellow."

"I promise," said the hunter, puzzled at the words.

With a nod, the tall figure turned and disappeared into the shadows of the forest.

The hunter spent the next morning looking for game, but again returned to his shelter empty-handed. The gnawing hunger in his belly reminded him that it was mealtime. It was time to make good his promise to his night visitor.

He had only traveled a short distance when he came to the stream, just as the stranger had described it. From the heavy growth on the north bank he heard a crackling and hissing like wind and rain. Listening, the hunter could make out the sound of bushes being uprooted and trees falling. Then he heard a similar sound from the south side of the stream.

Suddenly two huge snakes, each nearly a hundred feet long, burst forth from the underbrush—a yellow one from the north, and a white one from the south. They met in the middle of the stream and encircled each other with their powerful tails.

At first the hunter thought them evenly matched. Their coiled bodies churned the stream to muddy froth, while their immense tails lashed the water and bank with sounds as sharp as thundercracks. Neither seemed to have the advantage in the deadly struggle. Each opened its immense jaws as if to swallow the other, but now the yellow, now the white snake fended off the attack by twisting its body or using its own jaws.

Gradually, however, the white serpent seemed to weaken. The hunter, concealed a short distance away, decided that his visitor must have been the white snake changed to human form. True to his promise, he drew his bow and shot the yellow one. A second and third arrow also hit home, and the snake fell back, mortally

wounded. The swift-flowing stream soon carried it out of sight.

Then the white snake turned and retreated into the underbrush on the south bank. Not knowing what else to do, the hunter returned to his shelter to wait.

At dusk, his visitor of the night before came to thank him, saying, "You may stay here and hunt on this mountain for one year. From now on, you will find all the game you want. But I warn you: You must leave this place when one year has gone by. Never come again. If you do, bad luck will befall you."

"I promise," said the hunter.

With a nod, the tall figure vanished into the gloom.

It all came to pass as the snake had promised. From that moment on, the mountain woods and meadows provided the hunter with unlimited game, while the streams poured fish into his nets. Whenever he returned to his village, he would sell a portion of his bounty. Soon he became quite rich.

He marked the time carefully. When a year was up he came down from the mountain one last time, vowing never to return.

But as the years passed, the man was careless with his wealth. His money was gone, and his hunting and fishing barely brought him enough to eat.

At night, sitting in his hut, eating a bowl of watery rice with a single piece of fish in it, he would gaze into the distance at the forbidden mountain. He would see in his mind the glades where herds of deer grazed and the streams that teemed with fish.

Then he would remember the warning the strange visitor had given him, and turn away with a sigh.

But when there was nothing to eat except roots and bark, and his belly rumbled as loudly as mountain thunder, the hunter finally said to himself, "Surely enough time has gone by, and my hunger is so great, that the white snake would not punish me if I returned to the mountain for only one day."

The very next morning, he set out with his bow and nets. As soon as he entered the woods, he found the game as plentiful as ever. Soon he had a number of fat pheasants slung over his shoulder.

Suddenly, rounding a bend of the path he was following, he came face to face with the tall figure in white.

"Oh, my foolish friend!" cried the figure. "Didn't I tell you that you must never come here again? Now my enemy's sons have grown up. They are sure to take revenge on you, and I can do nothing to prevent it."

These words struck fear into the hunter. He begged the tall man to tell him how to escape.

"Too late," said the other, disappearing into the green shade of the forest.

At the same time, the hunter heard a sound like wind and rain moving through the trees toward him. Throwing aside the string of pheasants, he fled down the path.

For a time, the sounds kept growing louder. But he redoubled his efforts, until he was running faster than a startled hare. Gradually the sounds of pursuit began to fade. Finally they ceased altogether. With a cry of relief, he stumbled into a clearing, and realized that he was only a few paces from the edge of the woods at the foot of the mountain.

But when the weary man was halfway across the open space, three men dressed in yellow satin robes, all of them eight feet tall, suddenly slipped from the trees opposite him.

To his dismay, he saw their yellow garments slide off, like shed snakeskins. The three opened their impossibly huge mouths and kept on opening them, even as their hands and feet melted into their bodies, and their bodies lengthened and coiled.

The deer and birds, frozen in place, heard the sounds of three sets of powerful jaws clamping shut.

Then there was only silence upon the mountain.

The Draug

(Norway)

There are many stories told in Norway concerning the draug, a ghostly sailor with a mass of seaweed where his head should be. Sometimes he is no more than a menacing shape in a storm or mist. Sometimes he can be clearly seen as he sails his half-boat by night or swims in the ocean waters by moonlight.

The word *draug* means "a living dead person." Fishermen say it is the spirit of someone who was drowned at sea and who is now doomed to haunt the seaways, looking for victims to drag down and share his misery.

In 1864, in a small Norwegian village, the town magistrate, Ola Hagen; his wife, Solvy; and a crew of four oarsmen were charged with delivering a local criminal for trial. The court was in a town far down the coast.

They set sail in a small, open boat early on a September morning. The weather was fine, and they enjoyed a leisurely journey watching the unrolling panorama of steep, rock-walled fjords—many with waterfalls rushing down to the sea. From time to time they saw thick woods, or occasional patches of green farmland nestled beneath the cliffs.

Sturdy, good-hearted Solvy welcomed this brief escape from the duties of tending her house and vegetable garden. She sang sweetly as she kept watch over the waves ahead or spelled a rower at his oar. Her husband, Ola, leaning upon the rudder, skillfully guided the boat past the often treacherous rocks. He joined Solvy in a chorus, and their high spirits soon had the oarsmen singing, too.

Suddenly their prisoner, who had been lost in his thoughts, shouted, "Why are you mocking me this way? The devil take your accursed singing!"

Solvy said gently, "We were singing to pass the time— not to add to your troubles."

But the man said, "Bah! To the devil with every one of you!"

"Be quiet!" ordered Ola as Solvy blessed herself. She glanced around as though a horned devil might burst forth like a porpoise from the waves. Just to mention the evil one, she knew, might summon him. But the sea remained untroubled.

The prisoner turned away and said nothing more. But the pleasant mood was broken. They continued on their way in silence.

Toward evening, as they passed through a dangerous channel, they heard a forlorn cry.

"It's a seabird, nothing more," Ola assured his companions.

But his wife suddenly drew in her breath and pointed over the gunwale. To their horror, they saw a dark shape swimming around and around them. Abruptly it dove under the boat, setting the craft rocking to and fro. Then it shot from the water with a shriek and splashed back before any of the startled crew could see clearly what it was.

The boat was buffeted from side to side again. The youngest oarsman cried out, "Surely it is a draug who means to sink us!"

The craft pitched and rolled yet again.

"Come about!" ordered Ola Hagen. "We must head for shore!"

"Look! A light!" his wife said. "Perhaps there is a farm-house where we can find shelter for the night."

The four oarsmen bent their backs to the task, while the boat continued to rock as though in a storm. But the air was calm and the sky clear. If the frightened crew had not been rowing for dear life, they might have counted the glittering stars overhead.

When they entered a small inlet, their underwater tormentor suddenly left off its attacks. The boat sped smoothly across the sheltered water. In a moment they had moored their craft beside a fisherman's boat. Hurriedly, Ola and Solvy, the four oarsmen, and the prisoner in manacles hurried up the slippery path to knock on the door of a stone hut. From its single window, the butter-yellow light of an oil lamp streamed out to welcome the newcomers, who kept looking back over their shoulders at the still, starlit water of the cove.

Once only, a dark shape leaped out of the depths and back again—so quickly that Solvy, the only one who saw it, was not sure that she had really seen anything. But she shuddered nonetheless.

Then the door was pulled open. The fisherman inside, who recognized the magistrate and his wife, bade them all, "Come in."

When they had told their tale, the fisherman nodded and said, "On a moonlit night such as this, the draug shrieks so loudly that you may find sleep impossible."

After they had warmed themselves by the fire and had eaten some of the man's fish stew, the weary travelers settled down for the night on straw pallets beside the hearth. Though the walls of the cottage were solid stone, and the fisherman drew the shutters tight, none of the visitors was able to sleep. They were kept awake by piercing shrieks that continued until daybreak.

. . .

The travelers wearily shared some of their bread and cheese with the fisherman for breakfast, then continued on to their destination. There they turned the prisoner (who was only too glad to be away from the sea) over to the authorities. Because it was already late in the day, they decided to delay their departure until the next morning.

With fresh provisions and determined to return home before sunset, the six set out at dawn. As before, Ola claimed his place at the rudder, while Solvy took up watch in the prow. The steady rhythm of the four rested rowers and a full sail sent the small boat skimming across the waves.

But as the day lengthened, a strong headwind arose and slowed them. Soon, taking note of the westering sun, Solvy said, "I'm afraid we won't reach home before nightfall." Then she cautioned, "We should look for a place to tie up the boat and find shelter for the night."

Just then, however, the wind shifted in their favor. Ola said, "The breeze is helping us now, and the current is strong. I think we can still outrun the dark." So the oarsmen put even more effort into their rowing.

Indeed, landmarks along the shore showed that they were nearing home. With safety drawing closer, the youngest rower boasted, "I, for one, am not afraid of the draug. Let him throw his worst at me, I will throw it right back."

At that moment, the boat heaved as something large slammed into it from underneath. Shrieks erupted from the water all around them. The rowers strained at their oars, while the sail belled in the rising wind. But they were unable to make any headway. Something was holding them back.

"Something has fastened itself to the rudder!" cried Ola. At the same instant, a horrified Solvy, turning back to look at her husband, saw that water was pouring over the stern of the boat.

The sturdy mast groaned and seemed in danger of snapping as it resisted the sail's pull. The rowers churned the water with their suddenly useless oars. The boat remained in place as more water gushed over the gunwales.

"Ola! The boathook!" shouted Solvy.

Her husband grabbed the pole and began jabbing its metal point at the formless thing he could just make out under the surface. The sea seemed to boil all around the boat, and the air was filled with bloodcurdling screams. But the thing retreated from the sharp blade of the boathook. The vessel was released. It lurched forward, nearly pitching Ola out of the stern.

"Head for shore!" cried Solvy. "It's our only hope!"

For a few moments it seemed that they had escaped.

Then a black shape exploded out of the water beside the boat. In an instant it had seized the youngest oarsman and dragged him into the sea with a splash. His companions frantically searched the water for any trace of him, but all they could see was a circle of bubbles like tiny pearls, surrounding a single dark curl of seaweed.

The others reached shore safely, and huddled beside their beached craft through the night. In the morning, the survivors found their way home. Shuddering, Ola said, "The draug has claimed one victim. Let us beg merciful God that no others will fall prey to this horror for a long time to come."

The Vampire Cat

(Japan)

The prince of Hizen, in Japan, once fell in love with a beautiful and intelligent lady of his court named O Toyo. One evening, while the two strolled together in the fragrant palace gardens, the young woman noticed that they were being followed by a large black-and-white cat.

"How pretty!" O Toyo exclaimed.

But when she extended a hand to stroke the cat, it suddenly hissed at her, then ran away.

When they parted company a short time later, with soft murmurs of affection, O Toyo returned to her chamber. At midnight she was suddenly awakened by a strange sound. To her surprise, she discovered the black-and-white cat, grown to the size of a tiger, crouched in a corner, watching her. Before the frightened young woman could cry out, the creature leaped upon her. Breathing in, the demon cat drew the life out of O Toyo, and in an instant it took on her shape. Of the unhappy woman herself, nothing remained but perfumed ashes upon the bedclothes. These the false O Toyo blew upon and scattered.

In the morning, the prince greeted the creature whose soft voice, loving manner, and sweet laughter were O Toyo's in every regard. They talked of plans for their wedding. Every moment, the prince's love grew deeper and deeper.

But day by day, the prince felt his strength draining away. His face grew pale, his steps uncertain. He seemed to be suffering from some terrible, wasting sickness. The physicians and herbalists summoned by his councilors prescribed one treatment after another, but nothing helped. The young man grew ever more thin and ashen.

He suffered most at night, when his sleep was troubled by hideous dreams. They seemed so real that he told his servants, "Some demon slips into my chamber at night and steals a little of my life energy."

To ease their ruler's mind, his councilors appointed one hundred guards to sit up and keep watch over the sleeping prince. But curiously, on the very first night that the watch began, the guards were seized by drowsiness. Unable to keep their eyes open, they all quickly fell asleep.

In the morning, the councilors discovered to their dismay that the guards slept like the dead, and the prince had grown weaker than ever. The guards were punished for failing in their duty, and one hundred more were assigned to keep watch the second night.

But that night, the same thing happened. The prince was troubled by horrible dreams, while his guards slept helplessly all around him.

In despair, the councilors determined to sit up themselves, and see if they could resist the drowsiness that had overcome the prince's soldiers for two nights. Yet for all their determination, they fared no better. One by one they dropped off to sleep, long before midnight.

The next morning the prince was so weak he could not rouse himself from his bed. His three chief councilors met to discuss the problem, but they could arrive at no solution.

It chanced, however, that one of the palace guards, a young man named Ito, overheard their talk. Since it was clear that even the prince's wisest advisers were helpless, Ito determined to seek the advice of the priest at the city temple.

"Your purpose is a good one," said the priest. "But surely witchcraft is involved."

"If you will give me some way of resisting the drowsiness," said the young soldier, "I will sit up with the prince's guards this very night and try to discover the cause of his suffering."

Then the priest gave him a bit of parchment with a prayer inscribed on it. He said, "Recite these words softly if you feel yourself growing drowsy." Then he painted a magical sign on each of Ito's eyelids, to help him stay awake.

That night, Ito took his place amid the circle of guards surrounding the prince's bed at the center of the room. The ninety-nine others kept themselves awake with lively conversation or other amusements.

But as the hour of midnight approached, they began to doze off where they sat, in spite of all their efforts to keep each other awake. Ito also felt a great desire to sleep creeping over him, but he steadfastly prayed the sutra—prayer—the priest had given him.

His prayer and his strong will kept him awake, while the rest of the guards slept. Then, as he watched, the sliding doors of the prince's room parted. Ito pretended to be asleep, but he kept his eyes open just enough to see. To his amazement, he saw the beautiful lady O Toyo glide into the room. Cautiously she looked all around; when she saw that the guards were asleep, she smiled an evil smile and approached the prince's bedside. She knelt down as if she would kiss the sleeping man. But when her face was near his, she breathed in, drawing some life energy out of him.

At this, Ito stood up suddenly. The false O Toyo likewise rose, and turned to face Ito, who had his hand upon the hilt of his dagger. Ignoring the threat, she drew close and said, "I am not used to seeing you here. Who are you?"

"My name is Ito," he answered. "This is the first night I have been on guard."

"The other guards are all asleep. How is it that you alone are awake?"

"Prayer and a desire to help my lord," he said.

"You are a trusty watchman," she said. "I came to see how my lord fares this night. I will depart, knowing you are protecting him."

"You will not depart, goblin!" cried Ito, drawing his dagger. "I saw you stealing the life from my lord."

With a snarl, the beautiful woman was suddenly transformed into a monstrous cat that hissed and snarled and tried to rake Ito with its claws. But the soldier fought back with his dirk. For every wound the goblin cat inflicted, the man gave two in return. The sound of the fight began to rouse the sleeping guards.

Seeing that it was no match for Ito, and fearing the newly roused soldiers who were crying out alarms and drawing their own weapons, the giant cat suddenly fled the chamber.

Ito, yelling to the others to follow him, pursued the creature until it reached the gardens. It bounded to the rooftops and escaped over the palace walls. From there it fled to the mountains from which it had come.

From that moment, the prince of Hizen began to recover from his sickness, though he mourned the loss of

the beautiful lady O Toyo. When his strength was re-
stored, he raised Ito in rank to commander of the palace
guard and richly rewarded the young man.

For a time, reports came daily of the mischief the cat
was making among nearby villages. At last, the prince ordered Ito to lead a great hunt. After many days, the
soldiers cornered and killed the beast. Nor did any other
goblin come to trouble Hizen or its lord after that.

Windigo Island

(Canada)

Go steady wit' de oar!" shouted Cyprien Palache, leaning on the rudder. He was foreman of the crew of lumbermen paddling across Lake Manitou toward the island that would be their winter quarters.

The twelve men at their oars had been loudly singing "A-rolling My Bowl." But the cheerful refrain

> *A-rolly poley,*
> *My bolie rowlie*

had died away the minute the island came into view. The clouds above were motionless; there wasn't a ripple on the smooth lake. Yet it was said that even the strongest boats approaching the island were sometimes rocked by something unseen in the water.

Windigo Island was a hunters' paradise: Otters swam freely in its pools; muskrats built their mud houses and beavers their dams with little fear. The Indians never set traps there, though sometimes powerful medicine men would come to the island on secret and solitary missions.

The place was said to be haunted by a Windigo spirit. This frightful being may take many shapes—a giant with a heart of ice, a whirlwind, a demon, or a cannibal monster. Most of the men were unhappy about the choice of winter quarters, but none dared challenge the strapping, foul-

tempered Cyprien Palache. So they rowed on in silence,
listening for they knew not what.

They beached the boat on the rocky shore, under the
spruce and pine. Bawling orders and swearing, Cyprien
set the weary men to repairing the shanty built the previous year. They worked quickly, aware of the big foreman
watching every move with eyes as tiny and sharp as a wea-
sel's. If he saw a man doing something wrong or simply
pausing to catch a breath, he would roar, "Hi dere, w'at
you doin'?" and shake the unfortunate man until his teeth
rattled.

If the men who had aroused Cyprien's displeasure were
out of reach, he would sound a few shrill notes on the
silver whistle that hung from a chain around his neck, and
point at them in warning. The men hated the sound of the
whistle. The story was whispered around that Palache had
bought it in Quebec from the devil himself, who had used
it to pipe orders to the sinners in Hades.

When nightfall made work impossible, the men settled
into the cabin, happy to be away from the pooling dark
under the trees and the sound—so like soft voices—of the
rising wind in the leaves.

Their good spirits returned when, after supper, Pat
Clancy drew out his fiddle and Jimmie Charbonneau un-
packed his concertina. The two played, and all sang. But
Palache soon put a stop to the merriment, ordering the
men to bed and putting out the lamp.

Now, the youngest of the party was a Cree boy the men
called Indian Johnnie. The lumber gang had found him
half drowned in a river eddy the previous spring. His
mother and father had drowned when their birchbark canoe had been swamped by the swollen waters that followed the thaw. Somehow the boy had managed to keep

his head above water and swim free of the current. Palache treated him little better than a dog, using him as a servant and scullion. But the other men were teaching him the lumberjack's trade.

When the foreman wanted anything day or night, he would pipe three short blasts on his whistle, and Johnnie would come running. If the lad failed to appear before the whistle was sounded a second time, he would carry the bruises for days.

"How you stan' it?" asked Jimmie Charbonneau. "Why you never run away?"

But the boy just shrugged and said nothing. Jimmie knew that Johnnie would never let anyone see him cry. Still, he could see the hatred in the boy's face whenever the foreman appeared. Jimmie had the uneasy feeling that something bad was bound to happen. To his friend Pat Clancy he said, "Somebody surely die, long before de winter's over, long before we lef' dis place."

Pat only nodded grimly.

One morning after first snowfall, Jimmie noticed the boy burying something on the shore. Later, scraping away the snow, Jimmie found the body of a rabbit that the boy had caught the day before. Beside it was a little blue tobacco pouch. He didn't hear Palache come up behind him. "Hi dere, w'at you doin'?" snarled the big man, shoving Jimmie aside. "Dat's my t'bac!" he roared, snatching up the pouch.

He grabbed Jimmie by the collar, demanding, "Why you steal dis?"

Before Jimmie could say a word, the Indian boy, who had appeared from nowhere, grabbed Palache's arm. "I took dat."

"You?" the foreman said, releasing Jimmie and staring

at the Cree as though he had never really looked at him before. "Why?"

"For de *T'ing* dat's watchin', watchin' from de trees," said the boy, so softly the big man had to lean close to hear.

"What *T'ing*?" Palache snarled.

Jimmie realized then that the boy had left the rabbit and tobacco as a peace offering for the Windigo spirit. With a small shudder, he glanced right and left at the fringe of snow-dusted trees. "De boy mean de Win—"

But Johnnie suddenly reached up and stopped him from saying the word aloud.

"It ain' safe for told its name out loud," said Pat Clancy, who, with several others, had been drawn to the argument. "Dass de way it come—if it's call by its name."

At this, the foreman bellowed, "You can' all be such fools to belef' in Windigo!"

"Don' you say dat name some more!" yelled Clancy.

"Me, I say dat name all I wan'!" bellowed Palache. "Windigo! Windigo!"

Indian Johnnie groaned and clasped his hands to his ears.

"Enough dat!" The foreman dropped the boy with a blow to the side of the head. "De res' you fools get workin'. I don' wan' hear no more dis talk."

Then he stomped off toward the shanty, while the men scattered to their various tasks. Only Jimmie lingered long enough to help the dazed boy to his feet. But Johnnie just pushed his hand aside and walked away. Watching him go, Jimmie felt more sure than ever that there would be big trouble before the spring thaw.

December brought record snows. The drifts piled up so high against the cabin that sometimes only the roof and

chimney could be seen. Chilling winds hammered it con-
tinually.

One evening, as Cyprien was pulling off his snowshoes
and coat, he suddenly began to screech, "I los' my
whissle."

Jimmie and the others saw that the devil's whistle and
its chain were gone from around Palache's thick neck.

He grabbed Indian Johnnie and told him, "You mus'
fin' dat silver whissle an' de chain it's hangin' by, or don'
ever show yourse'f here again." Before anyone could pro-
test, the foreman thrust the Cree through the door into
the snow.

Now the wind outside grew louder. "Dat soun' lak
somet'ing cryin' all aroun' us ev'ryw'ere," said Jimmie
Charbonneau, shivering from more than cold.

Suddenly the fire in the stove dwindled and died.

"Charbonneau! Clancy!" yelled the foreman. "Go de
woodpile before I freeze to deat'." Palache, for all his blus-
ter, looked cold and white.

"Non!" said Jimmie. "We ain' afraid of not'ing, but we
don't like takin' chance."

"I hear some wil' spirit raisin' row dere," added Pat
Clancy. "You don't ketch us on no woodpile—no, siree!"

Nor would any other man budge from the circle around
the cold stove, in spite of Cyprien Palache shaking his
fist and threatening each in turn. Finally the big man
dropped onto his bed in the corner and simply glared at
his crew.

For a long time, nothing more was said. The men shiv-
ered and listened to the wind. Each one assumed that Indian Johnnie had been swallowed up by the storm—or
worse.

Jimmie dozed a little. Suddenly he awoke when he
heard something tap-tap-tapping at the window. He

turned and, through sleep-fogged eyes, saw a face at the window. At first he thought it was Johnnie, but then he realized the face was too big: It filled the window from side to side. And the eyes were like blue-black chips of ice.

He gave a cry, waking the others. But when they looked to where he was pointing, they saw only the frosty window glass, with a crescent of snow like a half smile across the ledge.

With a shaking hand, Jimmie wiped a circle in the frost. Beyond, he could see nothing but a pine stump in the clearing, like a tombstone rising out of the snow. For a moment he thought he heard—as though across a great distance—the voice of young Johnnie.

Then the shanty began to shake as the wind slammed it with the force of a hurricane. "De shaintee, she's gon' to fall!" cried Jimmie. Wind howled down the stovepipe, scattering ashes all around.

Suddenly there was a thunderous knock on the door, followed by three whistle blasts that cut through the howling wind.

"Dat Johnnie fin' my whissle!" cried Palache. He jumped up from his bed and yanked open the door.

Some men afterward said that the wind and swirling snow sucked him right out. But Jimmie Charbonneau swore that a huge hand, made of snow and tipped with nails of ice, grabbed the man and dragged him out into the storm. Then the door slammed shut.

By the time the lumbermen pulled it open again, not a trace of the foreman could be found.

In the morning, when the storm died away completely, the men found Johnnie, nearly frozen to death, huddled under the overturned boat. In the shelter of the tallest pine, Jimmie Charbonneau discovered the imprint of a single bare foot, with clawlike toes, about the size of a double sleigh. He called the others, but the wind and fresh-falling snow soon blurred the outline, leaving only a vague hollow in the snow.

Even Pat Clancy thought Jimmie had been imagining things. But Jimmie and Johnnie's eyes met, and they nodded to each other. They knew that Cyprien Palache had been carried off by a Windigo.

The Haunted Inn

(China)

In China long ago there was a young man named Li Wei, who was traveling with three companions. Early one evening, the four found themselves in a lonely countryside, with a storm beginning to break.

Hurrying along the road that was fast becoming a sea of mud, they spotted a small inn surrounded by willow trees. Delighted at their good fortune, they splashed across to the door. The innkeeper greeted them warmly, and his wife gave them welcome cups of steaming tea. But the newcomers quickly learned that many other travelers, also caught by the storm, had arrived before them. There was not a bed to be had—or even space enough for all the guests to stretch out on the floor.

The wife whispered something to her husband. He shrugged, then said apologetically, "The only space I can offer you is in the little building that stands some distance behind our inn. But I must warn you that the corpse of my daughter-in-law is laid out there. She died suddenly, and my son has gone to fetch a priest so that we may hold a proper funeral. He has not returned, and now I do not expect him until morning. You may all sleep there if you want to."

At first, young Wei hesitated. "It is surely unlucky to sleep in the same room as a corpse," he told his friends.

"That is true," one of his fellows agreed. "But what else are we to do?"

"I am too weary to argue," said Wei's second friend.

The third companion simply said, "Listen." The sound of rain battering the window lattices, and wind rattling the roof tiles decided the matter.

"Very well," Wei said to the innkeeper, "we will accept your offer."

So the old woman gave them mats to hold over their heads, while her husband guided the four travelers to the dark outbuilding that was set some distance from the house.

Inside, the innkeeper lit a candle. There was clean straw for bedding. At the back, a heavy curtain hid the unfortunate woman's body from view.

As soon as the old man was gone, the four friends settled down onto the straw. But while the others instantly fell asleep, Wei was troubled by the sense that something was amiss. He lay listening carefully, but he could hear only the rain pattering outside. The sputtering candle cast curious shadows on the pale curtain.

Then, with a hiss, the candle went out. At the same moment, Wei was sure that he could hear a rustling from behind the curtain.

Abruptly, the cloth was pulled aside. In the faint light seeping through the lattices, Wei saw the shape of a young woman, whose ghastly skin seemed almost to glow. Her nails looked as long as daggers.

Wei tried to cry out, but he was overcome by a listlessness that left him unable to move or speak. All he could do was raise his head slightly as he watched the form of the young woman bend over his companions. At first Wei thought she was merely studying each sleeper's features. But then he saw that she was breathing a greenish-white vapor into his friends' faces.

With a tremendous effort, he forced his hand inside his robe. There he grasped a bit of parchment on which his village priest had written magical Buddhist phrases to keep him safe on his journey. Though his every muscle seemed to resist, he managed to place this on his chest, just over his heart.

When the creature approached him just as she had approached his friends, Wei closed his eyes like one asleep. Every moment he expected to feel the touch of her claw-like nails or her chill breath upon his skin.

But after a short time, he heard the whisper of her robe going away from him. Opening his eyes a bit, he saw the figure gliding toward the back curtain. When she had passed into the alcove, she let the cloth fall back into place.

For a long time, Wei listened, but he could hear no further sounds from behind the cloth. At the same time, the listlessness left him, and he was able to sit up.

Hurriedly, he tried to rouse his companions. He whispered warnings and shook each of them, but to no avail. They were dead, killed by the woman's poisonous breath.

Suddenly he heard the curtain swept aside. He spun around and saw the woman coming at him, her claws outstretched like bundles of daggers. With a cry, the young man threw open the door and fled into the night. But in his haste he dropped his magic talisman.

Wei raced toward the inn and safety, half sliding down the muddy, tree-covered slope. Behind him he could hear the woman-thing in eager pursuit.

For a time Wei was able to use the willow trees as a screen, while he zigzagged away from his pursuer. But the creature quickly caught onto the trick, turned, and sprang at him, her extended nails aiming at his throat and heart. Wei was backed up against a willow tree. In desperation he threw himself sideways, tumbling into the mud. At the same moment, the woman's clawlike nails, driven by the weight of her body and the force of her leap, embedded themselves in the willow's trunk.

Wei staggered back toward the inn to rouse the inhabitants while the imprisoned creature struggled to break free.

When he told his story, he tried to convince the others to take up weapons and destroy the creature. But the innkeeper, his wife, and all the guests refused to do anything except bar the door and huddle together. Unwilling to face the monster alone, Wei joined the others as they watched fearfully and waited for the dawn.

Toward morning, the rain ceased. When the sun had fully risen, a few of the braver souls, led by Wei, approached the willow where he had last seen the creature. There they found the corpse, still fastened to the tree, dried to a husk in the sunlight.

When the innkeeper's son arrived soon after with a priest, certain rites were performed, and the body was burned. After that, the place was never troubled again. But Wei, for the rest of his life, refused to travel the road that ran past the willow-shaded inn.

The Rolling Head

(North America—Plains Indians)

There was once a warrior whose wife had died. He lived with his young son and daughter in a lodge apart from other people, near a forest at the edge of the prairie. For a long time the hunting was poor, and the family had little to eat save roots and berries. It saddened the man to see his children growing thin and ghostlike.

Now, it happened that his daughter had a gift of powerful medicine, as her mother once had. One night she had a dream in which a voice told her where a huge spiderweb could be found. "Tell your father to hang this web across the forest path where the animals go," the voice instructed her, "and you will no longer be hungry."

As soon as she woke, the girl told her father what she had dreamed. That very morning, he did what the dream voice had said. When he returned to the web in the evening, he found deer and rabbits entangled in its thick, sticky strands. These he took back to his children for food. Soon his son and daughter grew strong.

After a while the animals learned to avoid the web trap. From time to time the man was forced to move his snare deeper and deeper into the woods.

One day, after he had hung the web in a new place far from his lodge, he chanced upon a large lake, beside which stood a huge tepee, painted all over with strange designs. Uncertain whether to approach, he remained hidden by some brush.

Suddenly a tall old woman, three times the height of a man, pushed open the door flap. She walked to the edge of the water, where she whistled. In answer, the surface of the lake began to move and shake. Soon a monstrous snake rose from the waves and crawled out upon the land. Then the warrior in hiding knew that he had come upon the lodge of Snake Old Man and his ogress wife, Hungry Old Woman. The warrior was very much afraid, and hoped they would not find out he was near.

But Hungry Old Woman began to sniff the air. "Someone is near us!" she cried. "Catch him and put him in the cooking pot. I am so hungry, hungry!"

The snake slithered so swiftly toward the hunter that the man knew there was no hope of running away. He drew his knife just as the serpent wrapped itself around his body. All the while Hungry Old Woman cried, "Kill him quickly, so we can cook him!"

But the hunter thought of his children at home, who would be all alone if he perished. He fought as hard as he could, slew Snake Old Man, and cut the monster into pieces.

Then Hungry Old Woman gave a screech and ran after the hunter. He led her down the path that ran to the spiderweb. Behind him, he heard her jaws go *clack-clack-clack* as she tried to bite his elbows and heels. Then she was caught in the spiderweb. The ogress struggled fiercely, and had almost broken free, when the hunter struck off her head with his knife.

But Hungry Old Woman's body freed itself and began to chase him. Meanwhile, the head had smelled the children. Now it rolled out of the forest toward the lone tepee on the prairie. Inside, the girl was embroidering moccasins with porcupine quills stained different colors. Her little brother, who was gathering firewood, saw Hungry Old Woman's head rolling along the ground toward him, the teeth going *clack-clack-clack*. He ran away as fast as he could, crying, "Sister, I am being chased by a head!"

"Come inside!" his sister said, grabbing his hand. "Now close the tent flap." They fastened the hide flap with wooden pegs. The head rolled against the flap and partway up the tepee; then it rolled back down. Again and again it rolled against the hide, crying, "Children, children, open the door. I am hungry, hungry." The children knew it would soon split the side of the tent.

But the girl had a plan. She grabbed her quills and her root digger, a sharp-pointed stick. Then she told her brother to stand on one side of the tent opening while she stood on the other. She unfastened the pegs and drew the flap aside. Instantly the head rolled into the lodge and all the way to the back.

Then sister and brother jumped outside while the girl let the flap fall back into place. This kept the angry head inside just long enough for them to begin running across the prairie.

But soon the boy cried out, "Sister, I am tired! I can't run anymore!" The girl looked behind them and saw that the head had gotten out of the tepee and was rolling along the ground after them. Its hair streamed out behind it while its teeth went *clack-clack-clack*.

So the girl threw a handful of yellow porcupine quills on the ground, with a prayer to the Great Spirit. Instantly a great tangle of prickly pears sprang up behind them. These grew as tall as pines and were covered with great yellow thorns. They stretched for a long way in both directions.

When the head reached the thicket, its hair kept getting caught in the thorns, and it could not get through at first. But finally it chewed free with its sharp teeth, and rolled after the boy and girl, who had now run far away.

But soon they looked behind and saw the head coming

closer. Then the frightened boy called out, "Sister, I can't run anymore! Save yourself!"

Instead, the girl threw a fistful of white quills behind her, with a second prayer to the Great Spirit. Then there sprang up a range of mountains so tall that white snow topped them.

But the head found a nest of rattlesnakes, who were the cousins of Snake Old Man, and they showed her a tunnel through the mountain. Soon she had passed to the other side, and out onto the plains again.

On and on the children ran, but when they looked back they saw that the head was almost upon them.

"Sister, I am tired!" cried the boy. "I can't run anymore!"

Then the girl flung the blue quills behind her with a prayer. Where they fell, a great canyon opened. Far below, a river of swift blue water rushed through it. But, to her dismay, she saw that her brother, who had fallen behind her, was now on the other side. The rolling head was very close to him.

"Sister, help me!" the boy cried.

All she had now was her root digger. She laid this on the edge of the ravine, and it became a wooden bridge. Her brother ran across, and right behind him came the head, its teeth going *clack-clack-clack*. But the instant her brother reached her, when the head was still on the bridge, the girl shook the end of the root digger.

With a terrible shriek, the head tumbled down, down, down into the swift-flowing water, and was swept away.

Then they heard a shout and saw their father running toward the edge of the canyon; he was still pursued by the headless body. He ran right to the edge of the cliff. When the monster was almost upon him, he jumped aside. Unable to stop, the creature fell over the edge and into the river. In a moment it was carried away, just like the head.

The girl and her brother used the root digger to cross to where their father waited. He hugged them close. Then he picked up the weary little boy and, praising his daughter for destroying the ogress, led them back to the tepee. There they continued to live in peace, enjoying the plentiful game the spiderweb provided.

The Croglin Grange Vampire

(British Isles—England)

Croglin Grange in Cumberland, England, had been owned by a family named Fisher for over a hundred years. But in the last century they moved out and rented the house to two brothers, Andrew and Gordon, and their sister, Emma.

The threesome settled in easily enough, and soon made many friends in the neighborhood.

One hot summer day, when the sultry air made any kind of work impossible, the three dined early. Afterward they sat out on the veranda, savoring the cooling air, and watching the full moon rise and bathe the lawn and gardens in silver light.

At last they grew tired, and went indoors to their separate rooms. Emma found the night still too warm for sleep. Leaving her shutters open, and mounding the pillows behind her, she sat up in her bed, watching the moon through her ground-floor window.

Gradually she became aware of two tiny lights that flickered in and out of the row of trees that separated the Grange's lawn from the village churchyard beyond. At first they seemed nothing more than fireflies to the young woman. But as she continued to stare at them, she saw them drawing nearer. To her surprise, they seemed to be embedded in a darker shadow, which had detached itself from the moon-cast shadows under the trees.

Emma's hand went to her throat as she realized that *something* was approaching the house, and growing larger the nearer it came. From time to time the dark shape was swallowed up by the shadows of trees on the lawn. But it always reemerged, larger than before, and coming closer . . . closer. . . .

Emma was filled with horror; at first she wanted to cry out, but her throat felt paralyzed. Then she dreaded making the least sound or movement, for fear that the thing outside the French doors would be drawn by it. She was sure that the pitiful barrier of glass panes and thin wooden sashes would not deter it for an instant.

Suddenly, for no reason that the terrified woman could guess, the shape turned aside. She had the impression that it was going around the house, instead of moving straight toward her. The moment the tall, dark figure was out of sight, Emma leaped from her bed and ran to the hall door.

Just as her fingers circled the knob, however, she heard a blood-chilling *scratch, scratch, scratch* at the window. Turning, she saw a hideous brown face with flaming eyes glaring in at her. The thing rattled the French windows, which were securely locked on the inside. Emma was relieved to see that the flimsy-looking panels might keep it at bay. She tried to open the bedroom door to escape into the hall beyond, but the antique latch jammed, trapping her in the room.

The creature outside scratched again at the glass; then it began to peck with its nails at the sash. Emma saw that it was scraping out the lead that held the windowpanes in place. Again she tried to scream, but only a soft moan escaped her lips.

A single, diamond-shaped pane fell inward and shattered on the floor. A long, bony finger snaked through,

found the catch on the window, and flicked it open. Emma lurched toward the bed, hoping to reach the closet beyond. But the creature burst into the room, grabbed her hair with its long fingers, and dragged her down so that her head hung over the side of the bed. Then it leaned over and bit her on the throat.

The sting released her voice, and she at last began to scream aloud. As she struggled to push the awful face away from her, she heard her brothers shouting and banging on the door. At this, the monster suddenly fled from the room.

When Andrew and Gordon found the door would not budge, they slammed themselves against it, throwing it open by sheer force.

Inside they found their sister, bleeding from a wound in the throat and unconscious. Past the open French windows, nothing moved upon the moonlit lawn at first. Then Gordon cried, "I see him!" He pointed to a tall figure that fled from the shadows under a large oak. Without hesitation, he pursued it. But the monster moved twice as fast, with long, loping strides, and quickly leaped over the wall into the churchyard.

By the time Gordon had reached the fieldstone wall, he could see nothing beyond but gravestones and vaults. His quarry had vanished. Frustrated and angry, he returned to his sister's room.

There he found that Emma had regained consciousness, while Andrew dabbed at her wound with a damp towel.

"We shall keep watch the rest of the night," Andrew was saying. "In the morning, we will take the first train back to London."

"Andrew! Here's Gordon!" the young woman said. "Did you find out who—or what—attacked me?"

"No," her brother confessed, "it escaped into the churchyard. But, whatever the devil it was, Andrew is right: We must leave here as quickly as possible."

But Emma shook her head. "I will not let this experience drive us from the house where we have been so happy!"

Though her brothers tried to persuade her to leave, Emma refused. "We have leased this house for seven years," she said, "and we have been here less than one. We cannot afford to move elsewhere, while paying rent on this place."

Her brothers uneasily agreed with the logic of her argument. The next morning the local constable helped them decide when he suggested, "It must have been a lunatic, escaped from some asylum." Then he added, with great authority, "He is not likely to return."

So they stayed at Croglin Grange. But Andrew and Emma switched rooms. Emma kept her shutters closed fast at night, and each of her brothers kept a loaded pistol in his room.

The winter passed uneventfully enough, but the following March, Emma was suddenly awakened by a dreadful scratching at the shutters. Looking up, she saw the same brown, shriveled face staring back at her through the one pane at the top of the window left uncovered by the shutters.

She screamed as loud as she could, and her brothers rushed out of the house with drawn pistols. They spotted the creature loping away across the lawn. Andrew fired and hit it in the leg, but it got away, scrambling over the graveyard wall. This time the brothers reached the wall quickly enough to see the dark form disappear into a neglected vault.

．　　．　　．

The next day, in the presence of the tenants of Croglin Grange, the constable, and several other local authorities, the vault was opened. Inside they discovered that all the coffins had been broken apart and their contents scattered across the floor. Only one coffin lay intact, though its lid was loose.

Andrew and Gordon, at the constable's direction, raised the coffin lid. Then Emma gasped, for there, inside, was the brown and withered figure that had twice appeared to her at the Grange. Further investigation revealed that one leg of the corpse had been damaged by a pistol shot.

Though no one said the dreaded word "vampire" aloud, by common agreement they did the only thing that can lay such a creature to rest: They burned the body to ashes.

After this there were no more disturbances at Croglin Grange.

The Yara

(Brazil)

That part of Brazil called Amazonia, where the city of Manaus now stands and that is spanned by the Manaus–Caracarai Highway, once belonged to an Indian tribe. Jaguarari, son of the chief, was handsome and lithe as the spotted jaguar. He was fearless in the face of an enemy and was a bold, skillful hunter. When he paddled his canoe upon the Amazon River, the prow, lifted like a bird's wing, hardly seemed to touch the water.

At the celebration that marked the raising of youths to the status of warriors, everyone remarked on Jaguarari's pride of bearing, keen eye, and strength. His long arrow never failed to bring down the fleeing peccary or the bounding ocelot, while his blowgun dart dropped the preying hawk to the ground.

The young women dreamed that he would one day choose them for his bride; the old men boasted of his exploits; and his comrades sang songs that foretold how Jaguarari, on some distant day when his life was over, would climb the Blue Mountains, where the greatest heroes live for eternity.

Nothing pleased the young man more than guiding his canoe through the green shade along the river shore as he went fishing for *tucunare*, the slippery soapfish. He loved the solitude, when his only companion was a white-necked heron standing on a sandbar, or a flame-red parrot calling from the shore.

Jaguarari had always returned to his village at dusk, but there came a time when he began to stay on the water until midnight.

One night, after this had been going on for some time, his worried mother sat watching until she saw her son tie up his canoe. Then she followed him to his palm-thatched hut. There she found him sitting listlessly in his hammock, his legs dangling, his elbows on his knees. His eyes, dark-circled from sleepless nights and filled with sadness, were fixed on the black waters of the river.

Gently his mother asked him, "My son, what kind of fishing keeps you out on the water so late? Only evil spirits prowl the night."

But Jaguarari just sighed, and would not take his eyes from the river's edge.

"Son," the woman persisted, "what has made you so unhappy?"

Again, she got nothing but a sigh and a shrug for an answer. In the pale moonlight she saw that he had become as thin as a man suffering from a wasting disease or stung by a scorpion.

Deeply troubled, she left him as she had found him, his dark eyes locked on the equally dark river.

Jaguarari was soon spending all his time on the river. He refused to accompany his father, the chief, on a tapir hunt; Jaguarari often abandoned his comrades when they set snares for wild birds or cast fishing nets. They would watch him paddle his canoe up the river until he was out of sight, hidden by the tall trees draped with vines. Sometimes they would call to him, asking where he was going, but he never answered.

In desperation, his mother came to him and said, "My son, evil spirits surely have poisoned the air you breathe.

Your father has decided to move the village far away from here, so that you can breathe good air and be healed."

But Jaguarari only whispered, in a voice so low that she had to bend close to him to hear his words, "Mother, I saw her, floating among the water lilies in a distant lagoon."

"Son, who have you seen?" his anxious mother asked.

"She has no name," Jaguarari said, like one speaking from a fever dream, "but she is as beautiful as the moon. Her eyes are green as the skin of the *aruana* that swims at the mouth of the creek, and her hair is as gold as the morning sun shining on the river. She sings to me in a voice that is sweeter than any bird. My ears do not understand what she is singing, but my heart knows. Once, she made the water part, and showed me where she lives below. Someday I want to go there with her. Whenever I leave her, I want to see her again. I want to hear her song once more."

At this his terrified mother cried out, "My son, that is the Yara! You must promise you will never go back to that place. Death waits in her green eyes and her song!"

But her son only turned his face away, and would not speak to her any longer.

All the next day Jaguarari remained in his hut. His mother and father visited him as he lay listlessly in his hammock. But he would not answer his father's questions, or touch the smoked fish and fruit his mother left for him.

That evening his parents were suddenly drawn to the river's edge when a group of young women, who had gone to fetch water, cried, "Come, everyone! Come and see!"

The villagers stared open-mouthed as they saw Jaguarari, his canoe aimed at the red disk of the setting

sun, standing upright in the prow. His arms were outstretched like a bird about to take wing.

Beside him was the figure of a beautiful woman. Her
golden hair streamed out behind her, while her arms, as
pale as moonlight, were clasped about Jaguarari. She sang
a haunting song in an unknown language that momentarily stilled the twilight cries of birds and howler mon-
keys. Her song lingered in the hearts of all who heard it,
long after the sweet voice had passed out of earshot.

"The Yara!" sobbed Jaguarari's mother, turning her
face to her husband's chest. And though the chief and his
warriors tried to follow, and searched the river and every
lagoon and tributary for days to come, they found no trace
of Jaguarari or his canoe.

"Me, Myself"

(British Isles—Scotland)

Off the western coast of Scotland is a group of islands called the Hebrides, or "Western Islands." One of the largest is Islay, and near it is a smaller island, Orsay. For many years Orsay was used only for grazing cattle. These belonged to a laird, or landowner, on Islay, and were ferried across by boat, a few head at a time. The crossing was mild enough when the weather was clear and the sea was calm. Sailors knew to be careful of the fearful tides around the island, and only a foolhardy soul would attempt crossing the sound in bad weather.

Old stories said that Orsay was sometimes visited by kelpies, or water horses. These might emerge from the sea in the shape of horses or in the form of hairy, clumsy-looking men. People said that they could hear the kelpies wailing loudly near the island just before storms.

But the grass on the island was sweet and thick, and the laird would not let old stories keep him from fattening his herds. When all the cattle had been sent across, he hired a young man, Duncan MacPhee, and his new wife, Fiona, to tend his cattle. The two were very much in love, and needed only each other's company to be happy, so they got along quite well on the lonely island.

Duncan was a big, powerful man, with a handsome, weathered face dotted with freckles. Fiona was tall and fair-haired, with flashing blue eyes. At night, when the

cattle were safe in the byre, or cowshed, they would close
the shutters of the one-room stone cottage the laird had
built them. Then they would sit by the peat fire that
burned on the hearthstone in the middle of the dirt floor,
talking softly, while the wind howled outside the thick
stone walls and rattled the roof slates.

One afternoon, while they strolled along the rocky
beach, Duncan was delighted to discover four large eider
duck eggs. Fiona was far more excited when she found a
handful of "fairy eggs" nestled among the seaweed and
shells. These hard, light nuts, something like flat chest-
nuts, were gray, black, and brown.

"Ach, what are ye goin' to do with them sea nuts?"
asked Duncan.

"I'll string them on a bit o' ribbon," said Fiona, "to wear
'round my neck. My granny says they keep off the evil eye
and other wickedness. And cure sick cattle, too."

"Sure, they're not keepin' the kelpies away," said her
husband, pointing out to sea.

"Oh!" cried Fiona, clutching the fairy eggs to her chest.
As she looked out across the water, a brown head and a
gray head bobbed amid the waves. Two pair of soft, curious eyes met hers.

"Shame on ye, Duncan McPhee, for givin' me such a
turn!" she said. "Them's nothin' but two seals, wonderin'
what we're about."

"Ach, so they are. My mistake," he said, laughing and
taking her arm.

"Tease me so again," she said, with just the hint of a
smile, "and ye'll not think it near as funny."

At that moment, a fulmar gave a shrill, lonely cry, and
Fiona turned anxiously to look at the sea. But even the
seals had gone. There was only the empty expanse of
bright blue water.

"Tomorrow I must row across to Portnahaven for supplies," said Duncan as they climbed the steep path.

"Must ye?" she asked. "I feel a storm comin' on."

"There's precious few oats and barley left," he said, "and many other things we need besides. The weather will be fine, ye'll see."

Sure enough, the next day was mild, with calm and hazy sunshine over sea and land. Fiona rose early to cook barley bannocks. She wrapped the flat cakes of bread in some linen for Duncan to take with him. Standing on the bluff, she watched him rowing across the sound. Even as she gazed, she felt a wind rising, churning up waves. The little boat pitched and tossed, but Duncan was a skillful sailor, and he rowed on without mishap.

When she could no longer make out the rowboat, the young woman checked on the cattle, to be sure none was grazing too close to the cliff edge. Then she returned to the cottage, to feed the chickens and tend her little plot of turnips and potatoes. She kept busy, trying not to think of the changing weather. But when she stood up from digging in the garden, a strong, chill wind billowed her skirt and apron.

Looking toward the sound and the mainland beyond, she saw a heavy mist upon the dark blue sea. In a short time this gave way to a wind-driven rain. She prayed that Duncan would not be so foolish as to try to cross to Orsay in such foul weather.

When the cattle were secure in the byre, and the chickens in the hen coop, Fiona retreated to the cottage. She drew the shutters tight and prepared to sit out the storm, with a bowl of porridge and a cup of tea.

But while she was stirring the oatmeal with a spirtle, a wooden stick about a foot long, Fiona suddenly heard the sound of living creatures moving all around the house.

"Duncan!" she cried, thinking for a moment that her husband had returned and brought some other men with him. But the wail of the wind reminded her that the storm was too strong for Duncan to cross the sound.

"Sure now, it's the cows are out of their byre!" she exclaimed. She hurried to the nearest window and threw open the shutters. To her amazement, she found herself gazing into a pair of large, round, blazing red eyes that fastened on her own. The sight chilled her to the bone.

Gathering her wits, she pulled the shutters closed with a *bang* that set the dishes rattling on the shelf. In answer, she heard a low, whining laugh.

Too late, Fiona realized she hadn't barred the door. She reached up to drop the bar, but the door burst open. In walked an unearthly creature. He was very tall and large, and covered with rough hair everywhere except his face. This was covered with a dark, bluish skin that looked like fish scales. His long fingers were tipped with bone-white claws.

He lumbered to the fire and stared at Fiona, who stood just across from him. Between them the porridge bubbled on the hearthstone.

"What is your name?" he asked in the old language that Fiona had learned from her gran.

She answered the creature as confidently as she could, *"Mise mi Fhin,"* which means, "Me, Myself."

Suddenly the monster reached for her. But the brave young woman grabbed up the pot of boiling porridge with her apron and dashed it over him.

Yelling, the creature bounded through the door and into the rain beyond. Fiona heard a great babble of wild, growling voices asking in the old language what was wrong with their companion and who had hurt him.

"Mise mi Fihn! Mise mi Fihn!" he kept screeching. "Me, Myself! Me, Myself!"

At this, there arose a great shout of laughter. The rough voices taunted, "If you hurt yourself, then you must heal yourself."

Again there was brutish laughter. At this the girl rushed out and hid in the byre. She lay, sheltered by one of the cattle that had its back to the entrance. She touched her string of fairy eggs, hoping they might help keep her safe. Then she drew a circle around herself in the dust and prayed an "Our Father" in a whisper.

For a long time she lay shivering, hidden by the cow. Outside, the storm raged, and she heard the comings and goings of heavy footsteps. Several times she thought that one or more of the creatures had entered the cowshed, but she dared not peep around to see. She lay scarcely breathing.

As the storm grew wilder, the sounds outside turned to loud laughter, then fighting, as though the creatures had started a brawl among themselves. Fiona prayed that they would forget all about her.

Gradually the sounds of wind and rain and wild screeching began to fade. By the time that the first gray light of morning showed through chinks in the byre's rough stone wall, all was silent outside.

Making the sign of the cross, Fiona rose from her hiding place. She discovered that, though the consecrated circle had kept her safe, the cow that had protected her was dead; its back bore the marks of many claws.

The sea was calm and bright under the rising sun. Looking across the sound, she saw Duncan's rowboat on course for the island.

Her garden had been trampled by countless brutish

feet, ripping up her turnips and potatoes. Half-eaten remains were scattered all around. Inside, the spilled porridge was the only sign of the night's adventure. Shuddering, she drew on a shawl and hurried down to meet Duncan.

Though they were always on guard after this, and kept the shutters and door tightly barred after sunset, they were never again bothered by the kelpies.

Island of Fear

(North America—Seneca tribe)

There was once a young boy, Hatondas, whose parents had died. He lived with his grandparents deep in a great wood. Though they were loving and kind in many ways, they were always stern when they warned him, "When you leave our wigwam, do not go west."

Now, Hatondas was a good child, and for a long time he would explore only those forest paths that ran north and east and south. He would never venture into the dark shadows of the woods to the west.

But as he grew older, he became curious to know what might be found to the mysterious west. At last he decided to see what lay in this forbidden place. So, one morning, while his grandparents slept, he set out along the brush-choked trail that led west.

For a long time he could only advance very slowly, because the underbrush was too thick. Not even deer or other animals had worn paths through the wilderness. After a long, difficult journey, he came upon the banks of a broad, swift-flowing river.

"Is this what my grandfather and grandmother did not want me to see?" he asked himself. "Surely they have grown foolish in their old age."

He sat down very close to the water's edge to rest and to watch the shining river.

Suddenly he heard the bushes crackling behind him.

Then someone called out pleasantly, "Hai, Hai! Is this not a beautiful sight?"

Turning, Hatondas saw a handsome young warrior, his hand raised in a peaceful gesture. "Yes," Hatondas said to the newcomer, "I have never seen it before."

"Oh, then you must come with me to my canoe, not far from here," said the stranger. "I will take you to visit one of the islands nearby. We will return in a short time, and you will have seen many sights worth talking about."

Finding the young man pleasant company, Hatondas agreed. Together they walked to where a splendid birchbark canoe lay on the sandy beach of a cove. When they stepped into the canoe, the stranger gave a shove with his paddle and sent them into the current. With swift, even strokes, he quickly carried them far from shore.

Soon, a short distance ahead, Hatondas saw a small, pretty island with a dense clump of trees at the center. When they arrived on the beach of sparkling sand they both climbed out, and the stranger drew his canoe up on shore.

Beyond the beach grew masses of tall plants with blossoms as yellow as the sun. For a moment Hatondas drank in their beauty. But when he turned to look for his guide, the young man had vanished—and the canoe was no longer beached where they had left it. Amazed, Hatondas spotted the canoe far out on the river, halfway to the distant shore.

"Hai! Hai!" he shouted. "Come back! Come back!"

But the stranger would not look back. Realizing that he had been marooned, Hatondas sat down on a fallen log in the shade of some trees.

Suddenly he heard a whisper. "Boy! Boy!" The sound seemed to come up from the ground at the end of the log. There he noticed a small white spot. Scraping away at the

earth, he uncovered a skull. "Lift me into the sun for a moment," begged the skull. The whisper came from between the jaws, which never moved. "Let me feel its warmth again."

With shaking hands, Hatondas lifted the skull up to the sun. "Oh, how good! How I enjoy it! I am glad you found me!" the skull whispered. "Now I must warn you that this island is ruled by an ogre who commands powerful medicine. His son, who brings men across from the shore, only seems to be human. I was once a great medicine man myself. I came willingly to this island, thinking I would be strong enough to slay the sorcerer. But his magic was stronger than mine, and he killed me.

"He is gone away today, but he will return tomorrow with his son. Both of them eat men. They will gobble you up the way they did me and many others, unless you do as I tell you. If you heed me, you may escape and break the island's evil spell forever."

Frightened but courageous, the boy said, "I will."

"Before sunrise tomorrow, run to the beach where you landed and bury yourself in the sand so that only your eye and ear are uncovered. You must look and listen carefully, then tell me what you have learned."

The boy agreed to do this. Then he gently set the skull on a small hill, where it could enjoy the sun's warmth.

After a sleepless night, Hatondas went down to the shore at first light. He hid just as the skull had instructed him. Soon he heard the sound of singing from across the water. The song grew louder, and the boy, in hiding, guessed that the singer was approaching the island. Recognizing it as a song of power, Hatondas softly hummed it to himself, until he had learned it by heart.

Then he heard the crunch of the canoe as it touched the sandy beach. The singing stopped, but now Hatondas heard two voices: one, the voice of his young guide from the day before; the other, much older and rougher. The boy saw two ogres with horrible faces, pop eyes, and wide mouths full of sharp, yellow teeth.

"Well, where is my meal?" roared the taller of the two.

"I will fetch him," said the other. Though he no longer looked like the handsome warrior who had rowed Hatondas across to the island, his voice was the same. He vanished into the woods, while the other ogre tramped impatiently up and down the beach—often no more than a pace from where Hatondas lay hidden.

Finally the ogre son returned and said, "I cannot find him."

At this, the father stamped the ground and ordered his son to go and seek another victim. Then, grumbling, the sorcerer stormed through the woods, while his son returned to the canoe and hastened back to the mainland.

When both were out of sight, Hatondas uncovered himself and returned to tell the skull what he had seen and heard.

"You have done well. Now listen. First, go to the place where you found me, dig again in that spot, and you will find my medicine bundle. Bring it here."

The boy did as he was told, and soon uncovered a decayed medicine pouch. This he brought back to where the skull lay in a patch of sunlight. Then the skull whispered to him, "Make seven dolls from wood, and make a small bow and arrow for each. Cut the pouch into seven strips, and tie one strip around each doll. Then place them in the top of a tree near the beach. Hide yourself in the sand again at first light, and see what will happen."

The next morning the ogre son rowed across from the mainland, singing his song of power. When he reached the beach, he set down a bundle from which cries arose. Hatondas guessed that the ogre had stolen a baby. Suddenly, from the tree in which he had put the wooden dolls, came cries of "Ho-yo-ho!" When the ogre looked up to see what had made the sound, the tiny bowmen fired their arrows into the monster. From the way he cried out, Hatondas guessed that the sliverlike arrows had deadly power. Volley after volley flew from the tree. Soon the creature, bristling with arrows, fell in a heap on the sand.

Hatondas uncovered himself, grabbed the baby, and ran for the trees. When he glanced up at the dolls, he saw they were now only figures of dried wood. A moment later he heard the ogre sorcerer hurrying toward the beach. Clutching the infant, Hatondas hastened to the skull in its circle of sunlight.

Quickly, the boy told what had happened. "My magic is now finished," whispered the skull. "You must slay the sorcerer yourself."

"How can I do such a thing?" Hatondas asked.

"At the center of this island is a clearing. Within the clearing is the monster's wigwam. The creature leaves his heart inside so that he need not fear for his life. Destroy it, and you destroy the ogre."

Leaving the baby hidden beneath a bush, Hatondas hurried to find the huge wigwam deep within the woods. He thrust aside the entrance flap and saw, against the far wall, a large, beating heart. In the middle of the tent was a huge pot of boiling water.

Hatondas grabbed the heart just as the ogre came storming in. The creature snarled as he saw his intended victim holding his heart. Bellowing, the ogre grabbed for the boy, but Hatondas threw the heart into the bubbling water.

The monster gasped and screeched and then fell over backward. As his heart boiled away, so his very flesh boiled away, leaving only misshapen bones on the floor mats.

Hatondas took all the robes and blankets from the evil

wigwam, and set fire to it, so that nothing was left but ashes. Then he returned to where he had hidden the baby. The skull whispered, "When you destroyed the monster and his lodge, you broke the spell on the island. Go, take the child with you, and leave me here in the sunshine."

So Hatondas went back to the beach, took the ogre's canoe, and, singing the song of power, returned to his grandparents. They wept tears of joy to see him, because they thought he had been slain by a wild animal or drowned. Then they scolded him for going where they had told him not to go. But the boy apologized, and gave them the robes and blankets he had taken from the island, so they forgave his disobedience. Because they could not find out who the baby belonged to, he was raised as a brother to Hatondas. Now that the ogre was dead, they were free to follow any path they chose.

Three Who Sought Death

(British Isles—England—from Geoffrey Chaucer)

There were three reckless fellows in a tavern one day, who chanced to see a funeral procession passing by. They sent the tavern boy to inquire who had died. The lad returned and told them, "It is an old friend of yours, Forndronke, who was slain by the thief named Death."

"By heaven!" said the first fellow to his companions, "who is this Death that everyone is so afraid of him? Let us vow, on the spot, to go and find Death and rid the world of him before nightfall."

All three shook hands, and agreed to seek out Death and put an end to his work. When they asked the tavernkeeper where Death might be found, the man said, "Not far from here there is a village that has been ravaged by the plague. Men, women, and children, master and servant, have been claimed by Death. I am certain that you will find him there."

So off they went to find the unhappy village. But when they had gone only a little way, the three met a poor old man. They made fun of his long gray beard, his wrinkled skin, and the staff that he leaned on for support. They barred his path and would not let him pass.

"Please let me go my way," the old man begged. "For Death is following me, and I must outrun him to stay alive."

"No, old wretch, we will not let you pass," the three

said, "until you tell us where we can find Death. He has slain our friend, and now we mean to put an end to him!"

"Good sirs," said the old man, "if you want to find Death, look under that oak tree yonder."

At this, the three fellows let the old man go his way. They hurried to the tree, where they found not Death, but a chest filled with gold coins. Down they sat to count their newfound treasure, and promptly forgot their vow to seek out Death.

After a time the first man said, "We must be careful with this gold, or people will say we stole it, and hang us as thieves. Let us draw straws. Whichever of us draws the shortest will go to town and bring us food. The other two shall keep watch over the gold. Then, at night, we will each take away with us an equal part of the treasure, when no man can see us and accuse us of thievery."

This they agreed to, and accordingly drew straws. The shortest straw went to the youngest of the three. So they gave him a handful of gold coins, and off he went to town to get food.

Meanwhile, the two left guarding the remainder of the treasure decided that as soon as their fellow returned, they would kill him, eat the food, and divide up the gold two ways instead of three.

The youngest, as he walked to town, said to himself, "I could buy poison, and put it in the food, and slay my two companions. Then I would have all the treasure to myself." So he purchased a strong and violent poison, and put it in the food and drink he bought, and carried these to his fellows.

But his companions fell upon him and slew him the minute he returned. When they had buried his body, the first wretch said, "Now let us sit and eat and make merry, for we are wealthy men."

Then they ate the food their friend had brought, and quickly died from the poison in it.

So the three men found Death, whom they had been seeking, underneath the oak tree—just as the old man had promised.

Sister Death and
the Healer

(Mexico/American Southwest)

There was once a woodcutter, José, who fell asleep in the wood and did not wake until after dark. When he did, he met the skeletal figure of *Manita Muerte*, Sister Death, driving her wooden cart in which she gathers the souls of the newly departed.

"Buenas noches, señora," said the woodcutter respectfully, recognizing the figure who stood before him.

"Buenas noches, señor," Death replied. "Will you give me something to eat? The night is long, and I have grown hungry."

"Sí, sí!" said the woodcutter. He gave half of his rice and beans to her. "I am honored to share this, for I have long admired you. In a world that too much belongs to the rich and powerful, you play no favorites. All, rich or poor, will be taken into your cart sooner or later."

Now, Death was very pleased to hear him speak so. "I will give you any gift you wish for as a reward," she said.

"I have only one wish," the good-hearted man said, "that I might help those who are sick and suffering."

"Very well," said Death, "I will make you a *curandero*, a healer. All you must do is lay your hand on a sick person's brow, and he or she will be made well again. But you must *never* use your gift if you see me standing at the head of a sick person's bed. I will be there because God has decided to call the suffering one out of life. *No one* must keep me from gathering that soul into my cart."

The woodcutter readily agreed to this. With a quick nod of her head, Death sealed their bargain. Then she drove her cart away to the east, where the morning sun had begun to lighten the sky behind the mountains.

As José returned home, he wondered if he had had a waking dream. Surely, he told himself, he had not met *Manita Muerte* in fact.

Now it chanced that, on his way, he met old Luis, a friend of his. Luis was limping, because a burro had kicked him in the leg.

"Let me help you," José offered.

He started to put his arm around his friend's shoulder; but at his touch, Luis cried wonderingly, "My leg! You have healed my leg! How have you done this?"

Then José told the old man the story of his meeting with Death.

Astounded, Luis insisted on telling everyone they met about José's great gift. Soon young and old were coming to him, asking for his blessing and begging for his healing touch.

The new *curandero* used his powers carefully. Quite by accident, since his only goal was to help the sick and pain-ridden, the healer himself grew wealthy. Still, he remained a generous person, and gave away as much gold as he kept.

Then one day José fell in love with Dolores, the daughter of old Luis. They longed to spend every moment in each other's company. Often Dolores would accompany him on his healing visits. There she would comfort an anxious husband or wife, or take a tearful child onto her lap, while José prayed over the ailing person and worked

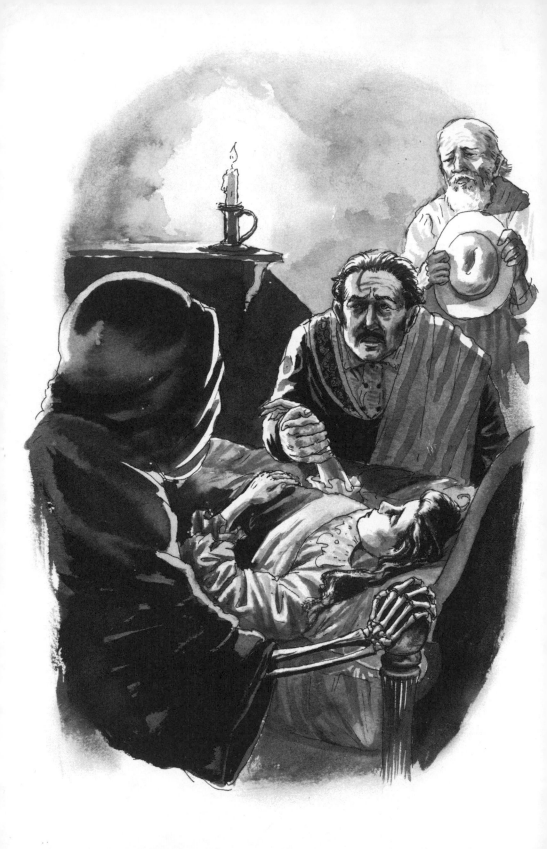

his wonderful cures through the gentle touch of his hands.

On the day before they were to be married, Dolores fell ill. When he was summoned to her bedside by her grieving father, José was distressed to see that Death was leaning upon one post at the head of the bed.

For the first and only time, José disobeyed *Manita Muerte*. He gently laid his hand upon Dolores's fevered brow and healed the young woman. At that instant, Death vanished from the room.

But as the *curandero* walked home late that night, Death's cart appeared on the road in front of him. When he dared look into the face of Death, he saw only a shadow underneath her cowl. He began to tremble.

Suddenly the moon and stars vanished. There was a moment of blinding darkness, and then he found himself in a cave filled with uncounted numbers of flickering candles. Death sat in her cart beside him. Slowly she raised a bony finger and pointed to a long and a short candle side by side on a nearby flat stone; the short one had almost guttered out.

"I warned you never to cure someone if I stood at the head of the bed, but you disobeyed me," Death said angrily. "Now you must suffer the consequences. Once you were the tall candle with a long life ahead, and the nearly extinguished one was your beloved. Your disobedience has reversed the two. Now *your* life candle is the short one."

"Have pity!" said the man, dropping to his knees and pleading with Death. "I did what I did because I couldn't live without Dolores, nor she without me."

"Then I will grant you one last mercy," said *Manita Muerte*. So saying, Sister Death leaned over and snuffed out both candles together.

In an instant, the dead man's soul was in the cart as it creaked and crept along the dusty road that leads to a distant, shadowed country. Beside him, in the silence, rode the soul of his beloved, as Death carried them out of the land of the living.

The Mouse Tower

(Germany)

In the middle of the Rhine River, near the city of Bingen, there has stood for hundreds of years a fortified rock topped by a large tower, called the *Mauseturm,* or mouse tower. Legend has long held that this was the scene of a terrible punishment sent by God upon a bishop who betrayed the faithful in his care.

In the year 970, Germany suffered from a terrible famine. In desperation, people were reduced to eating dogs and cats, and still countless numbers died of hunger. At this time, Hatto the Second was bishop of the region. Every day the starving poor would crowd around his door, begging for bread. It was widely known that he had plentiful supplies of grain set aside from the good harvest the year before.

But the bishop refused to part with the mounds of grain locked away in his bulging storehouses. His only thought was to increase his personal fortune.

From the high window of his palace, he would watch poor people fainting from hunger on the streets and storming the bread market, where they would take the bread by force. The bishop felt no pity at all for these starving people. But he soon grew weary of their cries day and night as they crowded around his palace walls, begging for a crust of bread, a handful of corn.

At last the bishop decided to quiet the mob. From his window he announced to them, "Let all you poor and needy gather in my great barn outside the city. There I shall feed you."

So it was that, from all directions, from near and far, a desperate army of hungry folk flocked to the bishop's barn. Loudly they sang the bishop's praises, while his soldiers urged them into the barn.

When the vast wooden structure could hold no more, the treacherous bishop ordered his soldiers to seal the doors. Then he had his men set fire to the barn, and burned the unfortunates, young and old, men and women. When the flames were at their highest, and the agonized cries were loudest, Hatto said, "Hear, hear, how the mice squeak! In faith, 'tis an excellent bonfire. The country is greatly obliged to me for ridding it of such mice who would only consume our precious corn."

The shouts and screams for mercy seemed to hang in the air long after the barn was reduced to nothing more than smoking embers.

Afterward, content with his day's work, the wicked man returned to his palace. There he sat down merrily to supper, and afterward slept the night like an innocent man.

But God soon saw to it that Bishop Hatto never slept again.

The very next morning, the bishop discovered his palace was infested with mice. They scurried down corridors and crawled over his feet while he took his ease or tried to read. They fouled the food in his larder and chewed his books and papers. They bit anyone who tried to drive them away. No efforts on his part could free Bishop Hatto from their torments.

When he entered his great hall, he discovered that mice had eaten his portrait out of its frame. The rectangle of splintered wood held only a few tatters of canvas. A short time later, a frightened farm servant reported to him that mice had devoured all the corn in his granaries.

Immediately thereafter, a second terrified messenger arrived and reported that a huge tide of mice was scurrying toward his palace.

Rushing to his window, the bishop could see the roads and fields dark with the advancing army. The vast horde of mice was chewing remorselessly through both hedge and wall, as the creatures made straight for the palace. The sound of their shrieking and squeaking chilled him to the heart.

Full of terror, Bishop Hatto escaped through the rear gate and commanded his men to row him out to his tower in the middle of the Rhine River. There he ordered his servants to bar every entrance.

But the mice followed him. They swam across the river, clambered up the rock, and crawled through every crack and crevice of the battlements. Swarming over the tower, they chewed their way in by the thousands, through oaken doors and plank floors and wooden ceilings.

And when they had cornered the wicked bishop, they climbed, dropped, and leaped upon him from all sides. As one old poem has it:

> *They whetted their teeth against the stones,*
> *And then they picked the bishop's bones;*
> *They gnawed the flesh from every limb,*
> *For they were sent to punish him.*

Then, as suddenly as they had appeared, the swarms of mice disappeared. Many people were convinced that the

animals were really the souls of those the bishop had so cruelly slain. The *Mauseturm* remains a place of fearful fascination. It is rumored that one can still hear the ghostly cries of the wretched bishop and the chittering of hordes of unseen mice on the anniversary of the fatal barn fire.

The Devil and Tom Walker

(United States—from a tale by Washington Irving)

A few miles from Boston, the sea has cut a deep inlet that winds several miles inland and ends in a thickly wooded swamp. On one side of the water is a dark grove of trees; on the opposite side the land rises abruptly from the shore into a high ridge, on which grow scattered oaks of immense age and size. Under one such tree, according to old stories, Captain Kidd the pirate buried a great treasure. The stories add that the devil oversaw the hiding of the money, and took it under his guardianship, as he always does with buried treasure that has been ill-gotten. Kidd never returned to claim his gold, being captured soon after at Boston, sent to England, and there hanged for piracy.

Later, in the year 1727, a miserly fellow named Tom Walker dwelled near this place. He lived in a forlorn house surrounded by a few straggling trees. One day Tom took a shortcut homeward, through the swamp. Like most shortcuts, it was an ill-chosen route.

It was dusk when Tom reached the ruins of an old fort in the middle of the swamp. He paused to rest on the trunk of a fallen hemlock. Absently, he turned up the soil with his walking staff. Suddenly his staff struck something hard, and he uncovered an ancient skull with a tomahawk buried deep in it.

"Humph!" said Tom Walker as he gave it a kick.

"Let that skull alone!" said a gruff voice. Tom looked up and saw a tall man dressed in black seated opposite him on the stump of a tree. He scowled at Tom with a pair of large red eyes. "What are you doing on my ground?"

"And pray, who are you, if I may be so bold?" said Tom.

"Oh, I go by various names. In this neighborhood I am known by the name of The Black Woodsman."

"If I mistake not," said Tom sturdily, "you are also commonly called Old Scratch."

"At your service!" replied the devil with a nod.

And so the two began a conversation as Tom returned homeward. The dark man told him of huge sums of gold and silver buried by Kidd the pirate, under the oak trees on the high ridge. This treasure was protected by his power, so that only someone who gained his favor could find it. This he offered to Tom, on certain conditions.

The conditions must have been very hard, because Tom asked for time to think about them, and he was not a man to worry about trifles when money was in view. When they reached the edge of the swamp, Tom said, "What proof have I that all you have been telling me is true?"

"Here's my signature," said Old Scratch, pressing his finger against Tom's forehead. Then he turned off into the swamp, and seemed to go down, down, down into the earth, until he totally disappeared.

When Tom reached home, he found a black fingerprint, which nothing could erase, on his forehead. This made him think even more carefully about the terms he had been offered.

Soon enough, however, greed won over caution. One evening Tom set out for the abandoned fort. Soon he met The Black Woodsman, with his ax on his shoulder, strolling through the swamp, humming a tune. By degrees Tom brought up the subject of business, and they began to haggle about the terms on which Tom was to have the pirate's treasure.

"You shall become a moneylender," the devil proposed. "You shall open a shop in Boston. You shall lend money to the desperate at ruinous rates, extort bonds, foreclose mortgages, and drive the merchants to bankruptcy—"

"I'll drive them to the devil!" cried Tom.

"Exactly," said the man in black with a grim smile. Then he extended his hand, saying, "Done!"

"Done!" said Tom Walker.

So they shook hands and struck a bargain.

Soon Tom Walker was seated behind his new desk in a countinghouse in Boston. The place was richly furnished, and had been paid for in antique gold coins to which traces of dark earth still clung.

His business was thronged by the needy who hoped to keep a roof over their heads and bread on the table; the foolhardy who dreamed of turning borrowed money into great fortunes; gamblers whose luck had run out; and merchants whose credit had dried up. In short, everyone driven to raise money by desperate means and desperate sacrifices hurried to Tom Walker.

Tom acted like a friend, but he always demanded full return and more for the money he loaned. He squeezed his customers as dry as a sponge, and sent them away destitute. In this way he became a rich and mighty man, and built himself a vast house.

As Tom grew old, however, he grew thoughtful. Having secured the good things of this world, he began to worry about the next. He regretted his deal with the devil, and tried to think of how to escape from his bargain with The Black Woodsman. All of a sudden he became a violent churchgoer. He prayed loudly, as if he could take possession of heaven by the force of lungs. He constantly censured his neighbors, and seemed to think that every sin he noted in them was a credit to him. Soon his zeal became as notorious as his riches.

In spite of all this, Tom dreaded that the devil would have his due after all and carry him off. So Tom always kept a small Bible in his coat pocket. He also had a huge Bible on his countinghouse desk, and was frequently found reading the Bible when people called on business. Then he would lay his spectacles in the book to mark the place, while he drove some ruinous bargain.

One hot summer afternoon, as a black thunderstorm was coming up, Tom sat in his countinghouse in his white cap and silk robe. He was about to foreclose a mortgage, which would ruin an unlucky man.

"My family will be driven to the poorhouse," the wretched man pleaded.

"I must take care of myself," replied Tom.

"But you have made so much money out of me already!" the other cried.

Tom lost his patience and his piety. "The devil take me," said he, "if I have made a farthing!"

Just then, there were three loud knocks at the door. Tom opened it to see who was there. A man dressed in a black woodsman's outfit was holding a black horse, which neighed and stamped with impatience.

"Tom, you're come for," said the fellow gruffly. Tom shrank back, but too late. He had left his little Bible in his coat pocket, and his big Bible on the desk, under the mortgage he was about to foreclose. Never was a sinner taken more unawares.

The black figure whisked him into the saddle, and the

horse galloped away down the streets. Tom Walker's white cap bobbed up and down, his robe fluttered in the wind, and the steed struck fire out of the cobblestones at every bound. The dark woodsman disappeared in a blaze of black fire.

Tom never returned to foreclose the mortgage. A man who lived on the border of the swamp reported that at the height of the thunderstorm he had heard a great clattering of hoofs and a howling along the road. He ran to the window and caught sight of a figure on a horse that raced like mad across the fields and down into the black swamp toward the old fort. Shortly thereafter, a lightning bolt fell and seemed to set the whole forest ablaze.

When neighbors searched Tom's offices they found all his bonds and mortgages burned to cinders. His huge iron chest was filled with chips and shavings of wood instead of gold and silver. The next day his house caught fire and burned to the ground.

Such was the end of Tom Walker and his ill-gotten wealth.

The Greedy Daughter

(Italy)

There once was a widow who had a daughter who was so greedy that the poor woman did not know what to do with her. She would gobble up everything in the house. When the widow came home from selling flowers in the market square, she would find nothing left to eat.

Now it happened that they had a wolf as a neighbor. The wolf had a frying pan, while the girl's mother was too poor to own one. Whenever she wanted to fry something, the mother sent her daughter, Filomena, to borrow the wolf's frying pan.

The wolf was very glad to loan the skillet to the widow. And he always sent a nice omelette in it so it would not be empty. The wolf intended this omelette for both mother and daughter. But Filomena was so greedy and so selfish that she always ate the omelette on the way home. Her poor mother never had so much as a taste.

When the good woman was finished with her frying, she would say to her daughter, "Filomena, in the morning scour the pan clean and return it to our neighbor. Take with you a loaf of the bread I baked today to thank him."

Filomena was lazy as well as greedy. She refused to clean the greasy frying pan. She waited until her mother had gone to the market square. Then she ate the loaf of bread meant for the wolf. After this, she took some mud, baked it in the fireplace, and put it in the frying pan. "Our neighbor is only a wolf, after all," she said to herself. "He will not know baked dirt from good bread."

The wolf was hurt when he saw the earthen loaf, but he was too good-hearted to say anything. After Filomena was gone, he said to himself, "Well, well! Perhaps things are going so badly for the widow that she can offer me no more than a bit of baked mud and ash. Next time they borrow the frying pan, I will make them an even finer omelette."

Soon enough, the old woman asked Filomena to visit the wolf and beg for the loan of his skillet. This time the wolf gave the girl the pan with an omelette so light and filled with fine herbs and cheese and ham that the greedy girl got only a short distance from the wolf's house before she gobbled up every bit of it. Not a speck was left for her mother that evening.

When the widow had finished her frying, she said to Filomena, "In the morning, scrub out the skillet and return it. And take with you this pitcher of cream to thank our neighbor."

As soon as her mother had left the next morning, greedy Filomena drank down every drop of the cream. Then she took the empty pitcher and the greasy frying pan with her and walked to the wolf's house. She paused on the way to dip up a pitcherful of ditch water, muttering, "Why waste sweet cream on a wolf? This will serve quite as well."

Again the wolf was offended by the sight of the greasy pan and the pitcher of ditch water. But he thanked the unkind girl anyway. To himself, he said, "Now things must really be desperate in the poor woman's house, that she can only send common ditch water by way of thanks."

Then he set to scouring the pan himself.

It chanced soon after this that the wolf met the widow in the market square. "How are things with you?" he asked.

"Well enough," she said.

"How do you like my omelettes?" asked the wolf.

"I am sure you make delicious omelettes," replied the confused woman. "But I have never had the pleasure of tasting so much as a mouthful."

"Never tasted them!" exclaimed the wolf. "How many times have you sent Filomena to borrow my frying pan?"

"I am ashamed to say how many times," said the flustered woman. "A great many, certainly."

"And every time I sent you an omelette in it," the wolf said.

"Never a bit of one reached me," the woman confessed.

"Then that greedy girl of yours must have eaten them on the way home every time."

Now the poor mother, anxious to keep the wolf from being angry at her daughter, made all manner of excuses for Filomena's greediness. But the wolf had grown even more suspicious, so he said, "The omelettes would have been better had the frying pan been properly cleaned before it was sent back to me."

"Surely you are mistaken!" cried the widow. "Filomena told me herself that she always cleaned it inside and out, until it sparkled as bright as new silver." Then, worried because the wolf was growing angrier by the minute, the good woman said, "I hope you enjoyed the little gifts of bread and cream I sent to you."

"Dirty ash and ditch water are all your wretched child brought to me!" cried the wolf.

"Dear neighbor, surely you are joking!" said the worried woman. "Perhaps I burned the bread myself. If there was water in the cream, then the farmer I bought it from was a cheat."

"Oh, I know who has been the cheat," said the wolf. "Now I must be on my way. Farewell."

So saying, he hurried away.

But he did not return to his own home. Instead he raced to the woman's house.

When Filomena saw the angry wolf approaching, she slammed shut the door. Then she called out, "Why have you come here?"

"I'm here to punish you for your unkind gifts of dirt and ditch water," he roared, "and your greedy way with the omelettes entrusted to you and the bread and cream that were meant for me!"

"Surely," the wicked girl cried out, "if anything is amiss, it was my mother's doing. She is in the market square. Go and gobble up that good-for-nothing if you must."

The wolf just growled and broke down the door. The frightened girl scrambled under the bed to hide herself, but it was as easy for the wolf to go under the bed as to get anywhere else. So under he went, and dragged her out, and gobbled her down on the spot.

And that was the end of the greedy daughter.

The Pirate

(United States—adapted from a poem by Richard H. Dana)

Near the close of the eighteenth century, a ship lay in a Spanish port, being outfitted for a voyage to America. One day, a Spanish doña, a widow, came to the dock, seeking passage to America. The unfortunate woman had no way of knowing that Captain Lee, grown weary of the poverty that dogged his life, had turned pirate.

Eyeing her fine dress, her golden rings, and her jewels, Lee offered her false sympathy for the loss of her husband and falser promises of a swift, safe passage across the ocean. Charmed by the captain's manner, the woman put herself, her servants, and all her wealth in the buccaneer's grasp.

At the very last moment—just before the ship set sail—the *señora* had her most prized possession brought on board: a milk-white Arabian horse. The stallion was tethered on deck. But from the first it stamped and reared and whinnied as though it sensed the danger hiding behind the captain's polite words and gracious manner.

As soon as the ship was out of sight of land, the crew, at a signal from Lee, slew all the lady's attendants as they slept. Then he and his men forced the door of her cabin open. It fell inward with a crash, but the lady fought the pirate with all her strength. She managed to break free of Lee's grasp and fled to the deck of the ship.

There, she tried to untie the Arabian as it raged against the ropes that kept it captive. Realizing that she could not free the horse in time, the brave woman drew her dagger and climbed onto the railing. Calling down the vengeance of heaven on the pirate who had betrayed her, she swore to battle to the end. Lee, tiring of the game, signaled one of his men to stun the frantic woman with a belaying pin, and take her prisoner. But in the confusion, the stricken woman fell backward, into the sea, with a dreadful shriek.

At the sound, the horse snapped its bonds and charged around the deck, trampling many of the pirate's men underhoof. Firing twice with his long-barreled pistols, Lee dropped the Arabian to its knees. Then he had his men throw the still-living horse into the sea.

For a time the stallion seemed almost to ride the swelling waves. Then it gave a cry unlike any heard by mortal men before. It rang out over the wide waters, causing even the fiercest pirate to shiver. Lee clasped his hands to the sides of his head and prayed he would never hear such a sound again.

For a time the cries continued, but they grew fainter as the milk-white steed was carried farther and farther away by the waves. After a while they blended with the cries of the ever-present gulls, and the pirate captain's moment of fear passed.

Then Lee divided up the *señora*'s gold. Several fights broke out over the division of the booty. "Avast!" Lee roared. "I'll have no more fighting on my ship!" He pitched one of his men overboard as a warning to the others. An uneasy quiet followed, for the men knew their captain would toss anyone who defied his orders to the sharks.

When they neared Block Island, off the coast of Rhode Island, Lee decided that his ship was too well known in the coastal waters of America. With the *señora*'s gold loaded into a lifeboat, he ordered the ship abandoned and set on fire. Then he and his surviving cutthroats rowed to shore. There they silenced any suspicious locals with a little extra gold.

Soon all but Lee drifted away to other ports and pursuits. With his stolen fortune, Lee no longer felt he needed the life of a pirate. He became a wealthy merchant, and began to woo the daughter of the town judge.

Exactly one year from the night when he had hurled a torch into the rigging of his pirate ship and rowed toward a new life with his stolen gold, Lee was walking along the shore toward his lady's house on the edge of town. Suddenly a glare lit up the sea, and he froze in midstride. Even more chilling was the unearthly cry that issued from the brightness—a cry Lee had heard only once before and had hoped he would never hear again.

The light on the horizon rapidly grew until it was the size of a rising moon, shooting streamers of milk-white and blood-red light across the waves. Now the man could see that it came from a ship, all on fire. Her hull was ablaze; each mast was a pillar of fire; her sails were sheets of flame. She raced shoreward with uncanny speed.

But faster yet came a ghastly white shape: a spectral horse's head rising from the depths. In an instant, the milk-white stallion had emerged from the water. It galloped from wave to wave as though it were crossing land. A moment later it reached the shore, and sped like the wind across the sand to where the hapless Lee stood watching in horror. Never once did the burning eyes— like twin coals in the beast's head—leave Lee's own.

When it was only a few paces from him, the horse stopped, snorting and stamping the ground impatiently. A power he could not resist forced Lee to mount the dreadful steed. The moment he was astride the devil horse, the creature carried him to the highest cliff of the island.

From here Lee could clearly see not only the burning ship, but also, in the water tinted white and red by the ghostly blaze, he could make out the bodies of all those he had slain. They rose from the depths, their arms outstretched to him, beckoning him into their midst. Clearest of all was the image of the wretched *señora*, whose pale, waterlogged skirts seemed to melt into the waves upon which she walked. She pointed her finger at him and smiled a grim smile that turned his insides to ice.

"Have mercy, I beg you!" cried the former pirate.

But the horse shook its head as if it understood his plea. To his horror, Lee saw there was no mercy in the faces of his ghostly victims. With a shudder, he remembered that he had not shown any one of them mercy. All around, the night was filled with their calls: "Join us, join us, join us."

But more terrifying yet was the *señora*. As if his fright were some vast joke, she threw back her head and laughed. At first the sound was as shrill as a seagull's call— but it quickly deepened until it became as loud as the howl of gale winds that would tear a ship apart on the open sea.

Then the ghostly woman made a single gesture with her hand and vanished in a spout of flame.

Suddenly the specter horse leaped into the air and plunged down through the night air as if it were a steep slope. Across the sand it galloped while Lee twisted and cried out in wild despair.

But he was bound to the horse by some fearful spell. Soon the steed was racing across the water lit by the burning ship. All around Lee, half-submerged figures clawed at his boots and clutched at the tails of his coat.

On and on the demon horse rode, until the fiery hull

rose before Lee like a curtain of flame. With an anguished cry, he flung his arms over his eyes.

There was a final burst of twining red and white flame that lit the sea from one end of the island to the other. Then horse and rider, ship and ghosts vanished—extinguished as suddenly as a candle flame.

There was only an expanse of shadow-dark waves rolling endlessly, endlessly shoreward.

The Golden Arm

(British Isles—England)

There was once a handsome but miserly man who traveled far and wide in search of a wife. He cared little that a woman was young or old, pretty or plain, sweet-tempered or shrewish—he only insisted that she be rich, not poor.

At last he found a beautiful woman who was raven-haired, blue-eyed, and rosy-cheeked, with lips as full and ripe as cherries. She had been born without a right arm; but her father was so rich, he had had the finest goldsmith in England fashion her an arm of gold. It was this and her own fortune that made the miser decide to marry her. In truth, he was fonder of her golden arm than of all his wife's other gifts combined.

At first the young woman was in love with her husband, and dreamed that her good nature would sweeten his sour disposition. But his greed and miserliness soon turned her as sharp and bitter as himself. They spent long days and longer nights arguing. Whenever it seemed that she might go away and leave him, he would stroke her cheek, pat her golden arm, and promise to mend his pinchpenny ways.

But he never did. Again and again she would threaten to leave, but she never did. As time went on, the man grew even more tightfisted with their money.

In the depth of winter, his shivering wife said,

We have no wood,
We lack for coals:
Outside the winds howl like lost souls.
Husband, dear, I beg you, please,
Let me buy fuel before we freeze.

But he answered,

Wood and coal cost more each day.
I will not pay and pay and pay,
And so throw all my wealth away.
Not one penny will you get today.

When their underfed horse no longer had the strength to pull their ancient carriage, his wife pleaded,

Our starving horse
Is skin and bone.
Our greaseless carriage wheels groan.
Husband, dear, I beg you, please,
Let me buy some oats and grease.

But all he would say was,

Oats and grease cost more each day.
I will not pay and pay and pay,
And so throw all my wealth away.
Not one penny will you get today.

They had no food in the larder, and hunger made the poor woman frantic. She begged,

Our tea is weak,
Our soup is thin,

We live on crusts and turnip skins.
Husband, dear, I beg you, please,
Let me buy some meat and cheese.

But his answer was always the same,

Meat and cheese cost more each day.
I will not pay and pay and pay,
And so throw all my wealth away.
Not one penny will you get today.

Soon his wife grew sickly from lack of food and from loneliness. She would sit by the cold hearth, the fingers of her hand of flesh twined around the fingers of her golden hand, listening to the wind whistle up and down the chimney.

Her husband often sat beside her, just as silent, his eyes drawn always to the golden arm, which seemed to grow more beautiful every day, while her other arm wasted away.

Finally she took to her bed, knowing she would not rise from it again. Her husband sat beside her, stroking the golden arm, while she said:

Husband, as my last request,
I charge you: See that I shall rest
For all eternity
In the gown I wore as bride
With my golden arm beside,
Then shall I slumber peacefully.

He nodded and patted her golden arm. Then she sighed and closed her eyes a final time.

.   .   .

After she was dead, her husband put on his tall black hat and long black coat, and even managed to have a few tears in his eyes when he met his wife's family at her funeral. When she was laid to rest in the churchyard, he wept as though his heart were broken.

But as soon as the other mourners were gone, in the dead of night, he returned to the churchyard. There he dug up his wife's coffin and took her golden arm. Then he hurried home with his ghastly treasure, certain that no one would ever know what he had done.

To keep the golden arm safe from thieves, he hid it under his bed pillows. For two nights he fell asleep, dreaming dreams of golden kingdoms.

But on the third night, just as he was drifting into sleep, he suddenly woke up, thinking he had heard footsteps on the staircase.

> *I locked the door with special care,*
> *Surely there is no one there,*

he told himself as he drew the covers up to his chest.
    He heard the sound again, a step or two higher.

> *That's just a mouse upon the stair,*
> *Surely there is no one there.*

But he drew the bedclothes up to his chin all the same.
    A third time he heard the sound.

> *A drape was moved by restless air—*
> *Surely there is no one there,*

he whispered. Then he drew the blankets up to his nose.

One more time he heard the faint sound of a footstep;
now it was just outside the door to his room.

Mustering all his courage, he said aloud,

> *I have no reason to beware:*
> *And yet I must know,* Who is there?

At these words, the ghost of his dead wife glided into the
room. She stood at the foot of the bed and stared at him
reproachfully.

Pretending not to be afraid, he spoke to the ghost, saying, "Your raven hair's grown lank and gray."

She answered, "The grave has stolen its sheen away."

"Your hollow eyes brim with dismay."

"The grave has stolen my joy away."

"Your cheeks are marked by sad decay."

"The grave has stolen their bloom away."

"Your gown is stained with moss and clay."

"The grave has stolen its beauty away."

"Why have you left your grave this day?"

"To fetch my arm you stole away!"

At this, the man cried out, and backed away from the
ghost, as deep into the pillows on his bed as he could. But
before he could deny the theft, he felt fingers—hard as
steel, cold as the grave—wrap around his throat.

In a moment there was only silence.

In another moment,

> *There was a footfall on the stair,*
> *A gleam of gold,*
> *Then nothing there.*

The Serpent Woman

(Spain)

Long ago, in Spain, near the city of Cordova, there dwelled a man named Don Juan de Amarillo. Though he was far from young himself, he had a handsome young wife, Doña Pepa. No one knew where she came from: All anyone knew was that Don Juan had gone traveling for many years, and had returned with a new wife.

There was something uncanny about her perfect features, dark eyes, and skin as pale as marble and as cool to the touch. Her tall, thin form was strangely flexible and lithe. Though all Don Juan's friends were charmed by her beauty and elegant manners at first, they soon went out of their way to avoid the lady.

There was a *strangeness* about her. When pleased, she swayed her body to and fro with delight. If she was displeased, her head seemed to flatten out, and the touch of her hand was like a bite. She delighted in spreading gossip about her neighbors, whether they had offended her or not.

To all appearances, Don Juan adored his wife. But the servants whispered that they argued from morning to night, and that Don Juan seemed deathly afraid of Doña Pepa—especially when her head flattened in anger. Stories circulated that she was a sorceress who had bewitched the unhappy Don Juan.

. . .

Because Don Juan and his wife had no children, the old man decided to leave his wealth to his poor nephew, Don Luis, of whom he was very fond. He invited the young man to come from Aragon for a visit.

Don Luis was an honest, open-hearted young man who quickly became popular with his uncle's servants and friends. Only Doña Pepa disliked him. She seemed disgusted that people should discover that Don Juan had such poor relations.

Whenever she saw the young man, she would smile politely if anyone was watching. But when only he could see, she would shoot him a look of such scorn and hatred that he shuddered. At such moments her head flattened, her eyes grew long and narrow, and she moistened her lips (white with rage) with a hissing sound.

Don Luis lived in constant fear of her, and kept out of her way by every polite means. But she would not let him escape, and always revealed a little more of her hatred to him. He was sure that she hoped to drive him away from his uncle's house and his inheritance. Yet, for love of the kind Don Juan, the young man said nothing.

One night, returning from a visit to a friend, Don Luis lit a candle and headed toward his room. As he walked down the hall, he stumbled over what he thought was a coil of rope. To his horror, the rope uncoiled itself, and a large black snake glided upstairs and disappeared under his uncle's door.

Fearing for Don Juan, he pounded on the door until his uncle opened it and demanded crossly, "Why do you disturb my sleep in the middle of the night?"

"I saw a large black snake creep under your door, my dear uncle," the young man hastily explained.

"Nonsense!" exclaimed Don Juan, turning pale. "There is no serpent here."

"I insist on searching your room," said Don Luis.

"Very well," said his uncle, "but be quick about it."

Don Luis searched everywhere but found nothing. He was so quiet that he did not awaken Doña Pepa, who slept on until the moment he was leaving. Then she suddenly opened her eyes; her head flattened, and her eyes grew long and narrow. The young man quickly left the room with many apologies, but his dreams that night were filled with loathsome snakes.

The next morning, Don Luis found only his aunt when he went down to breakfast.

Doña Pepa stared at him coldly. "I warn you, nephew, you do not belong here," she said. "If you stay, I will teach you the true meaning of fear."

As she said this, she seized him by the wrist. He felt a stinging pain. He threw her hand aside and hurried out. But by the afternoon his arm had begun to swell and throb, until he had to go to the doctor in town.

The doctor examined his arm, noted a wound on his wrist, and said, "That is a serpent's bite."

"No," said Don Luis, "my aunt grabbed my arm in anger."

"I can give you medicine for the bite," said the doctor, who had met Doña Pepa many times. "For the rest, you will have to decide your own course of action."

The two men shared a glance of deep understanding.

That night, as Don Luis climbed into bed, he found the black snake coiled by his feet. Instantly he drew his sword and struck the reptile, cutting off a piece of its tail. The snake reared its head and bared its fangs, preparing to strike. But Don Luis slashed another piece off the tail. Hissing, the snake flowed to the door, then under it.

Don Luis followed it upstairs and saw it disappear under Don Juan's door. Don Luis did not alarm his uncle this time. He decided that the snake had a hiding hole in the wall or floor of the room and would remain hidden from any searchers.

The next morning, Doña Pepa did not appear. "Your aunt has a habit of sleepwalking," Don Juan explained to his nephew. "Last night she stepped on something sharp."

For days, Don Luis did not see his aunt. When she reappeared, she greeted him politely enough, but he noticed that she walked with a limp.

That night, Don Luis was surprised by the snake, which had hidden in a corner of his room. Only his quick reflexes saved him. He spun away from the deadly jaws, grabbed his sword, and struck the creature a few inches below its head. The wounded snake escaped before he could strike it again. When he looked down the hallway, he could see no trace of the thing. But he was sure that it had fled to its secret hiding place in his uncle's room.

For a month afterward, Doña Pepa kept to her darkened room. His uncle explained that she had fallen victim to a fever that required her to rest and avoid all company. At last, looking paler than ever, she appeared and accompanied Don Juan on an errand to Cordova. As she passed Don Luis, her dark eyes flashed with such hatred that he felt it like a blow.

When they were gone, he began a search of their room, determined to find out the secret of the black snake. He looked everywhere, but found nothing. Then, in a chest under a window, he discovered a skin striped like a serpent's. He guessed that the snake had hidden in the chest long enough to shed its skin.

Don Luis was taking the unwholesome thing downstairs when he heard his uncle's carriage returning. Since it was evening, the great fire in the main hall was burning. Without a thought, the young man threw the skin on the fire. It blazed, then quickly crisped and curled into nothing.

Suddenly there was a great commotion at the front door. Servants ran to and fro as Don Juan came in, carrying Doña Pepa, who had fainted. They set her on a couch, where she lay looking very pale and ill. A man was sent to fetch the doctor.

"What happened, dear uncle?" asked Don Luis.

"I don't know, I don't know," his uncle answered. "We had just stepped from the carriage when your aunt suddenly screamed that her skin was on fire. She began to twist about and beat her hands upon her skirt as though it were in flames. A moment later, she fell into my arms."

Don Luis glanced at the fireplace, where not a trace of the snakeskin remained. He remembered his mother telling him, when he was a child, "God sometimes punishes an evil woman by making her become a snake every night for a number of years equal to her crimes."

His thoughts were interrupted when the doctor arrived. He rushed to Doña Pepa's side, took up her hand, and felt for her pulse.

"What is the matter with her?" asked Don Luis.

"She is dead," replied the doctor.

Though Don Juan was genuinely saddened by his wife's untimely death, it seemed to his nephew that a burden of worries had dropped from him. His uncle's friends, arriving to offer comfort, commented that they had not seen the old man looking so well in years.

For a time, Don Luis concerned himself with setting his uncle's affairs in order. He began to think that his aunt's death at the moment he burned the snakeskin was merely an unhappy coincidence.

Then one morning the old woman who was his uncle's most trusted servant confided in Don Luis. "You know, *señor,* I prepared Doña Pepa for burial. While I was busy at my sad work, I saw the figure of a large snake traced upon the length of her body. Was that not strange?"

"Indeed," said Don Luis. "My aunt, God give her rest, took many secrets with her to the grave. And that, I think, is best for all of us."

Loft the Enchanter

(Iceland)

In the Middle Ages there was a boy named Loft, who chose to study magic, learning certain small spells and charms from a hermit who lived in the wilderness a distance from the village. It was rumored that the man had once been a great sorcerer but had lost most of his skill—and his senses—when he probed too deeply into the shadowy world of magic.

"Have a care, Loft," his neighbors warned, "or thou wilt suffer the same fate. Or a worse one!"

But the young man only laughed at them. "I will become the greatest wizard of all," he boasted. "I will hold the most powerful spirits in my hands."

When the good pastor of the village urged him to change his ways, Loft grew angry. He caused a monstrous shape to appear and frighten the pastor's horse while he was crossing a stream swollen with snowmelt. The pastor was tumbled into the raging water and barely escaped with his life. Thereafter, the clergyman offered prayers for Loft's soul but stayed out of his path.

In time, Loft traveled far to the north, where the most powerful sorcerers in the region kept a school for the study of the black arts. There he increased his skills and learned the dangerous secrets of the terrible book called *Greyskin*. In this, the greatest wizards and warlocks of the past had written down many of their most potent spells.

His unceasing pursuit of dark secrets turned his mind to wickedness. While he was still a student he punished a fellow student, a bully who had beaten him. Using magic, Loft created a doorway in a solid wall. From within came elfin music and sweet singing. When the curious boy stepped through it, the wall flowed back together, trapping him forever in the stone. The mystery of his disappearance caused great puzzlement, and more than a little suspicion was cast on Loft. But the young man denied any knowledge of the missing pupil's whereabouts.

Greedy for even more knowledge and power, Loft vowed to conjure up the ghost of the mightiest sorcerer of old, Gottskalk the Cruel. He hoped to compel that spirit to hand over the legendary book *Redskin,* which had been buried with the magician in his secret grave. In this book Gottskalk had gathered the most fearsome spells of old.

On a moonlit night, Loft barred the door to his tower room and began the conjuring spell. But as soon as he started, a voice moaned, "Cease, while there is still time."

"I will not," Loft answered boldly. He continued about his evil business.

A second time the voice warned, "Cease! There is but a little time to save yourself."

"Silence!" Loft commanded.

When Loft had fully cast his spell, the ghost of Gottskalk appeared. The figure was tall and lean, with burning eyes and skin as gray as the grave.

"Thou hast chanted well enough," said the spirit, "for all that thou didst stumble over certain words."

"I command thee, hand over the book *Redskin,*" ordered Loft.

"Upstart," growled the specter. "Dost thou dare to treat me like some mere apprentice? Though thou study for a hundred times a hundred years, thou shalt never force me to surrender *Redskin* to thee."

"Give it here," Loft persisted, extending his hand. "As I have summoned thee, thou must do my bidding."

By the flickering candlelight, the ghost began to grow huge until it bent double at the ceiling. "Arrogant fool," the monstrous shape said with a laugh, "thy doom is sealed, because thou hast tampered with power thou cannot begin to understand."

Then the ghost began to laugh again. The sound was so loud that Loft pressed his hands to his ears. All the while, the vast gray figure continued to grow and swell, until it filled the room and forced Loft out onto the stairway landing.

Standing upright, the ghastly giant pressed its shoulders against the ceiling beams. The wood snapped and masonry rained down as it lifted the roof off the tower.

Loft fled, but the booming laughter followed him down the winding stairs. Suddenly a great foot thrust down through the overhead wreckage and tried to smash him like a bug. Loft threw himself out of the way, tumbling down the remaining steps and landing, bruised and dazed, at the bottom.

He forced himself to his feet, while the whole tower around him heaved and shook as in an earthquake. Walls cracked and falling dust nearly blinded him. From outside he could hear alarms and the cries of masters and students.

Loft stumbled to the stable, saddled his horse, and fled the sorcerers' school. Behind him a voice roared, "Run to the ends of the earth or cross the seven seas, thou shalt *never* escape my vengeance." Then came peals of titanic laughter.

Loft lashed his horse and sped away until the thunderous laughter dwindled to an echo in his ears. The night grew silent.

He rode west for several days and nights. Finally he took refuge in a small hamlet called Stadastadur, where green hills sloped down to the sea. The simple houses built of rough blocks of lava with roofs of turf were a far cry from the grand halls of the school.

Here he found the pastor kindly disposed toward him. The old man charged Loft with the upkeep of the church and grounds; in return, he promised to help Loft study Scripture.

For a long while, Loft refused to leave the blessed grounds of the church. At night he stayed indoors and would only read his Bible and pray.

But in time his fear subsided, as one day became the next and there was no sign of punishment from beyond the grave. At first Loft only dared to venture into the village on errands. Later he would sometimes stroll the outskirts of the town, or go for longer walks in the countryside.

"I have escaped the doom that Gottskalk pronounced on me," he decided. "Whatever power I gave him that night must have faded with the dawn. He cannot reach me in my new life here."

One sunny day not long after this, when the sea was calm and the sky was clear, Loft decided to row out into the cove to do some fishing. Several locals who happened to be gazing seaward later reported to the pastor that they had seen his boat bobbing on gentle waves in the windless afternoon. And they had recognized the figure of the assistant pastor fishing.

Then, to their horror, they saw a huge arm, gray as the

grave and covered with dripping seaweed, rise up out of the sea. It grabbed the boat by the stern and, in a trice, pulled it under the water.

No bit of wreckage—not so much as an oarblade—floated back to shore. Nor was Loft ever seen on earth again.

The Accursed House

(United States—Ohio)

An old farmhouse belonging to a man named Herman Deluse once stood near Gallipolis, Ohio. Though he paid scant attention to his fields or livestock, and the house was little better than a ruin, the old man never lacked for anything. He kept to himself, and discouraged his neighbors from visiting.

Many people suspected that Deluse had been a pirate. He called his place the Isle of Pines, after a notorious gathering place for buccaneers in the West Indies. On those rare occasions when the Reverend Henry Galbraith and his son William visited—the only two callers Deluse would tolerate—the man made no attempt to conceal the strange objects from distant lands and curious weapons that filled his house.

As William grew older, he asked more and more questions about the old man's source of wealth. The boy was sure that Deluse had pirate treasure hidden in the house. Though the old man never appeared to have much money at one time, he always had enough to meet his needs. And he always paid for things with old Spanish gold pieces. This convinced the people of Gallipolis—and young William in particular—that he was a former pirate. Some even suggested that he had moved so far away from the ocean because there was a price on his head.

But all William's efforts to get the old man to reveal the

source of his gold failed. Deluse remained tight-lipped, never providing any clue as to the whereabouts of his treasure—if, indeed, it existed.

When it came time for Deluse to die, he passed away alone, and was buried quietly in the nearby cemetery. Isle of Pines was locked up, while inquiries were made to determine if there were any relatives to claim the estate.

Now, it chanced that while this was going on, the Reverend Galbraith was away for a month-long visit to Cincinnati. He did not know that Herman Deluse had died. One night he returned home in the middle of a terrible storm. The snow was so deep and the road so blocked with drifts and fallen branches that he looked around for shelter.

To his relief, he saw a light. He followed it through the driving snow and recognized the Isle of Pines. As he neared the place, he noted that the light was moving about the house, brightening one darkened room after another. Whatever could old Deluse be up to? he wondered as he knocked. When no one came to the door, he rapped again even more loudly.

But still he was ignored, as the light moved from chamber to chamber. Finally, afraid of freezing to death, the reverend put his shoulder to the door and forced it open.

"Hello, Herman!" he called. "I apologize for my rude entry."

But when the old man at last appeared, carrying a candle, he paid no attention to the clergyman. Instead, he wandered about like a sleepwalker, muttering to himself, searching for something. His visitor tried to strike up a conversation, but Herman persisted in running his hands over each wall, then dropping to his knees and searching the floor.

"What have you lost?" asked the concerned Reverend Galbraith. "Can I help you search?"

Still the old man would not look at him; rather, he carried his candle to a room at the end of the passageway. In the chilly darkness, the reverend could hear him muttering over and over again. The sound made the reverend as uncomfortable as the cold. To ease his mind and body, he set about building a fire in the fireplace. Then, spreading his coat before it, he lay down, intending but a few moments' rest.

Instead, he fell into a deep sleep that lasted the better part of the night. The first light of dawn was just visible through the thinning snow when Reverend Galbraith was roused by Deluse's triumphant cry, " 'Tis here! 'Tis found!"

Pulling his coat around him, the clergyman hurried down the hall to the little room at its end. He was sure that was where the cry had come from.

But when he entered the room, he found no trace of Herman Deluse. Against the northern wall was an unlit candle stub in the curious holder that the old man had carried during his midnight search. In the dust that coated the wall, he could just make out the impression of two hands, as though someone—old Deluse, surely—had pressed his palms against the surface.

More puzzled than ever, Reverend Galbraith called out his friend's name. But though he searched from cellar to attic, he could find no trace of the man. The doors and windows were all shut tight. Nor, as he peered through the early morning dimness, could he see any footsteps in the newfallen snow.

Daunted by this mystery, Reverend Galbraith took his horse from its shelter in the tumbledown barn and continued the rest of the way home, the storm having fully abated.

.   .   .

He was welcomed by his wife and son and a good friend
—a lawyer named Maren—who had come by on some bit
of business that morning. But when he told his story, his
wife and son merely glanced at each other, while the lawyer remarked, "Didn't you know that Deluse was dead
and buried?"

The clergyman, speechless, merely shook his head.

"You must have been dreaming," said his son. But William's eyes shone with a curious light.

Reverend Galbraith insisted, "I tell you, it happened
just as I said."

"If you like," said the lawyer good-naturedly, "we will
go there tonight and investigate. Perhaps the ghost will
appear again after dark."

"Play the fools if you want!" exclaimed William, adding,
"I have business on the other side of town. I won't be back
until supper."

By nine o'clock, when the lawyer came by to accompany
Reverend Galbraith to Isle of Pines, William had not returned. "I'm relieved he isn't here," the clergyman confessed to Maren. "He seems to have no patience with talk
of ghosts."

Together they rode out to the farm. Just as the clergyman had reported, the two men saw a light appearing first
at one window, then the next. But when they drew near,
the place went suddenly dark.

The front door stood open. "I know that I locked it
securely when I left," said Reverend Galbraith.

Inside, all was darkness and silence. The men had
brought candles, which they now lighted. In the thick dust
on the floor they saw the marks of the clergyman's stay
and his footprints. A second set of footprints led purpose-
fully from the front door down the hall to the little room

at its end. The door, which had been open that morning, was now shut. Flickering candlelight shone beneath it.

"Someone else has been here since you left," said the lawyer. "And I believe he is still here."

Suddenly from behind the door came a scream, then the sound of a heavy body hitting the floor, then silence.

Trembling, the two men hurried down the passage. Inside the little room they found the northern wall broken open. From the hollow space behind it several pouches had spilled their golden contents, while just below, William Galbraith lay sprawled on the floor, covered with antique Spanish coins.

With a cry, his father stooped to pick him up, then staggered back in horror, for the young man was cold and dead.

A postmortem examination revealed no cause of death, and a jury issued a verdict of death due to a "visitation of God." But Reverend Galbraith remained convinced to the end of his days that his son had been frightened to death by something quite *un*godly in that accursed farmhouse.

Escape up the Tree

(*Nigeria*)

There was a young man, a hunter, who had some power with charms and magic. Each day, when he set out into the forest, he would place a bowl of water in the sun. Then he would tell his mother, "If this water turns the color of blood, you will know I am in danger. Then you must unchain my three dogs and send them to rescue me."

The old woman always promised that she would do as he asked.

Now it happened that, one day while he was hunting, the young man came to a nearby village. There he found a crowd of people watching as all the unmarried young men tried to toss *ege*, tree seeds, into a hollow calabash shell. Behind the gourd knelt the most beautiful woman the hunter had ever seen.

When the young man asked what was going on, he was told that the woman had promised to marry whichever man could toss the most *ege* into the calabash.

Thinking to try his luck, the hunter took his place at the proper distance from the gourd. The woman glanced up at him and smiled. Now he was more determined than ever to win the contest. Carefully he tossed the seeds one after another into the calabash. Every seed hit its mark, a feat no one else was able to match.

At last the headman of the village declared that the

hunter had won the contest and earned the woman's hand.

She came to him shyly, but when he asked where she lived, she only said, "A great distance from here."

"Then I will take you with me to my home," the man said, "where my mother will welcome you like a daughter."

Now, despite the hunter's skills with magic, he did not realize that the young woman was really a she-devil. She had come to town seeking to lure away a man so that she could satisfy her hunger for human flesh.

After they had walked for a time, the young woman said, "Let us stop in this clearing and rest awhile. I have grown very tired."

Indeed, the young man was feeling weary himself, so he was quite willing to sit down with his back to a tree. Across from him, his bride-to-be sat watching him, smiling and licking her lips.

His eyes closed. He slept. Then an insect stung him on the shoulder, waking him. The woman across from him was no longer a woman. She was changing into a big mass of red eyes and sharp teeth.

Instantly the young man jumped up and climbed into the lower branches of the tree, just as the horror rolled across the clearing toward him. Dozens of sets of teeth snapped at his heels as he scrambled higher and higher.

Now, the she-demon could not climb the tree, but she set to work chewing the trunk, determined to topple it. The hunter recited one of the magical chants he knew, and ordered the tree to grow higher while the trunk grew thicker.

At this, the monster roared in anger. "Whatever power you have," the many mouths said together, "it will not be enough to escape me. You are going to die. I will pick your bones clean and then grind them to dust!"

So saying, the she-devil redoubled her efforts to topple the tree. Again and again the hunter used his chant, but each time he found his magic had grown weaker. The tree would grow only a tiny bit higher; the trunk would thicken only a little more.

"Why have my dogs not come to rescue me?" he wondered.

Now, his mother had taken some clothes to the stream to wash them, so she had not seen the water in the bowl turn blood red. The dogs, sensing something was amiss, were howling and trying to burst their chains. Finally the old woman at the riverbank heard them barking. Gathering up her washing, she ran to the hut.

The moment she saw the blood-red water bubbling in the pot, she gave a frightened cry. Then she unchained her son's three dogs. Instantly they raced into the woods. They reached the clearing just as the mass of teeth, busy at the base of the tree, had bitten almost all the way through the trunk.

The three huge hounds attacked the monstrous thing from all sides. As they worried it, and chased it away from the tree, the hunter slipped down and recovered his spear, which he had left lying on the ground. The dogs had already badly wounded the demon, so the hunter was able to kill it with a single thrust of his spear.

The rolling eyes grew dark; the snapping teeth were stilled; the thing shuddered and died.

Then the hunter returned home with his three dogs. There his mother, overjoyed to see him safe, prepared a great meal, to which she invited all their friends. And the hunter's three faithful dogs ate as well as any of the guests.

The Headrest

(Papua New Guinea)

In the old days, it happened that Inay, a man from the hills, came to a certain village, leading his little son by the hand. He spent the day trading with the villagers and talking with them. His boy, Mimau, sat beside him, silent and smiling shyly. People remarked what a well-behaved child he was—a blessing to his father and mother. The women kindly gave father and son taro, bananas, plantains, and sugarcane to eat.

When darkness fell, the stranger went into the *potuma*, the common house, where the men slept, to spend the night. He took his son with him. But in the *potuma* was Kakak, a man of the village who was short-tempered and violent. When he saw the hill man's child about to fall asleep beside his father, Kakak raised a great cry. While two of Kakak's friends held the hill man in check, the angry villager shook Mimau. "What are you doing here, boy?" he cried. "Don't you know that this is a house for men? Go away at once!" Then Kakak beat the little child and shoved him out of the door into the dirt beyond. The boy lay still; his spirit had fled his body.

Inay also was expelled from the *potuma*. When he saw the lifeless form of his son, he gave a cry that echoed from the distant hills. Then wordlessly, he gathered the body of his little Mimau in his arms and walked away into the night. At this Kakak boasted, "That is how I will deal with all strangers who do not respect our customs." Then, contented, he lay down to sleep.

Only a few days after this it happened that all the people of the village were fishing at the river, so no one noticed Inay creep into the empty *potuma*. When the hill man entered, he carried something in his hands; but when he left, his hands were empty. Still unseen, Inay hurried back to the hills.

At evening, the men of the village returned. After they had eaten, they went into the *potuma* and made ready to sleep, for they were weary after a day spent fishing. In the center of the sleeping place, Kakak saw a headrest carved of wood. Instantly, he claimed it for his own, saying, "This is my pillow. If any of you wish it, you must take it from me in a wrestling match—if you dare."

But the other men, knowing his fierceness and strength, refused to wrestle with him. They just shrugged and let him be. Then Kakak lay down, rested his neck on the carved wooden headrest, and was soon asleep.

In the morning, the men awoke, stretched, and one by one came out of the *potuma* into the village. But Kakak was not among them. It surprised the others that he was still sleeping, for he was usually the first to arise. After a time, one man went in and tried to rouse the fierce man. But when he looked closely, he saw that Kakak was dead. Then he made a great outcry, calling to the other men. When they saw the body, the men were very much afraid. "How could he have died so quickly and quietly?" they asked each other. "Surely he was bewitched."

Kakak was buried, and his name was no longer spoken aloud, as was the custom when someone died. But the man who had first tried to wake him took the headrest for himself. It chanced that he was one of the two who had held back the hill man while Kakak beat his child. That night he lay down to sleep. And in the morning he also was found dead.

"What evil comes into the *potuma* at night that kills men so swiftly?" the villagers wondered fearfully. "Let us watch all through the night to see what shape our enemy takes."

So the men sat up all through the night, but they saw nothing. In the morning they went wearily about their business, unsure whether the evil had truly gone away, or was merely waiting to strike again when they might be less watchful.

In the warmth of the afternoon, one man crept back to the *potuma* to sleep, while all his fellows were fishing. As it happened, this was the second of the two men who had held the hill man while his child was beaten. Seeing the headrest in a corner, he placed it under his neck, sighed contentedly, and was soon fast asleep.

Now his fellows, noticing that he was gone from the riverbank, sent a boy to fetch him. The child had just reached the entrance of the *potuma* when he saw the headrest slide out from under the sleeping man, fly into the air, then fall with great force on the sleeper's head. The man lay dead upon the ground, with the headrest beside him, before the child could so much as cry out a warning.

Fearful that the thing might fall on his own head, the boy ran back to the river, shouting to tell everyone what he had seen.

For a long time the men remained outside the common house, staring at the slain man's body and the headrest beside it. After much discussion, they gathered as much wood as possible and built a great fire in the open space outside the *potuma*. Then the strongest and bravest man went inside and picked up the headrest. To the touch, it seemed nothing more than ordinary wood. But when he neared the bonfire, the headrest began to twist about in his grip, as though it would break free.

With a cry partly of fear and partly of disgust, the man cast the headrest into the hottest part of the flames. Instantly, the wood caught fire. Then, as the villagers watched aghast, it writhed and crawled about the pyre as if it were truly alive. All the while it groaned, "A-ge-ge-ge-ge-ge!" and screamed, "A-ke-ke-ke-ke-ke!" until it was burned to ashes.

Then, from the heart of the dying fire arose a whirlwind. It carried the ashes of the headrest high into the air. There other winds caught them and carried them across the river and over the trees toward the distant hills and a village high in the mountains. They would be a sign to Inay, watching silently from the door of his hut, that vengeance had been exacted for the violence done to his little son.

The Thing in the Woods

(United States—Louisiana)

Once, in the Louisiana backwoods, there was a Cajun woman, Odette, who wanted nothing more than to have a child. But God had not granted her and her husband that gift. Sometimes she would be going about her housework when she would pause and gaze into the yard, imagining a child playing there. Her husband, Alcide, would often say, "I wish I had a son, me. That boy, when he grow up he would be best hunter in whole bayou country and Unite' States, him!"

Poor Odette spent most of her days in church, praying to the Virgin Mary. "Please let me have a *bebe* for Alcide," she would plead. "I promise I would love that child so."

But no child was sent to them.

Now, there was a stretch of woods haunted by the evil one, the devil himself. People were safe as long as they stayed on the path that ran through the forest, but they risked their lives and very souls if they strayed into the trees on either side.

When Odette was a little girl, her mother had often warned her, as she set out to school, "You be careful, Odette! You keep your feets on the road, yes. Don't you go wandering off after a flower or nothing. You walk straight to the schoolhouse and don't pay no mind to nothing else!"

But now, one spring day, as Odette was walking to church along that very road, she spied a beautiful flower growing right beside the path. It had long white petals surrounding a center as red as the finest ruby. So perfect was it that it might have been fashioned by an artist instead of growing wild. A little ways beyond it, she saw another such blossom and another.

"I will take these to church and give them to the Virgin Mary," she said. "Maybe then she will give me a *bebe*, yes?"

So she began to gather a bouquet, and didn't notice that each flower she picked led her deeper into the woods.

Suddenly she heard a sound like a child crying. Looking around anxiously, she spotted something blue under a tree. It was a bundle wrapped in blankets, from which came the child's cries. Instantly Odette dropped her flowers and ran toward it.

Swaddled in the sky-blue cloth was a handsome little baby boy, with skin as white as milk. As she reached down and gently lifted the infant in her arms, he laughed and gurgled in a way that went straight to her heart.

"Has your careless mother left you all alone here?" she asked the child. But the *bebe* only laughed and cooed even louder. Then Odette said to herself, "Maybe the Virgin has answered my prayers by sending me to find this child. I will take him home, yes. He will be a son for Alcide."

With the child gathered in her arms, the young woman hurried out of the woods. But as she neared the road, she remembered she had not thanked the Virgin for giving her this son. She carefully spread out her shawl in the shade of a tree. Upon this she gently set her blue-wrapped bundle. Then she knelt to pray.

But as soon as she had uttered the first words of her prayer, the infant began to yell and shriek. At first she tried to pray in spite of his cries. But he screamed louder and louder, almost as if her prayers were causing him pain.

At last Odette whispered to the Virgin that she would say her prayer of thanksgiving when she got home. "Let me get this *bebe* some milk and put him to bed. Then I'll pray some more, me," she promised.

So she started to pick the little one up. She raised the corner of the blanket that covered his face to speak a soothing word to the squirming baby. But when she did, her heart turned to ice.

No perfect infant with milk-white skin was in her arms. Instead she was holding something that was all black and shiny and ugly—like some beetle. And even as she watched, the thing began to grow, getting bigger and bigger by the minute. Poor Odette was so frightened that she nearly died on the spot.

She dropped the writhing bundle on the ground. To her horror she found she couldn't move: Her legs felt like they were rooted to the spot. Not knowing what else to do, she made the sign of the cross in the air over the tangled blanket, from which two shiny black claws had emerged.

To her everlasting relief, she found that she had done the right thing. The evil one hates the mark of the cross. The creature that was still half hidden gave a yell like forty devils. Then Odette saw something that looked partly like a giant beetle, and partly like a little hunched-up man with shiny insect skin, run off into the woods.

As soon as its cries had died away, Odette found that she could move again.

Still shaking, she hastened directly to the church, where she thanked God and the Virgin for her escape.

The very next day, Alcide and Odette moved far away to Bayou Barataria. There they made a new life for them-

selves, and in time they were blessed with a family of five sons and four daughters. Odette was careful to see that each child said his or her prayers day and night, went to church faithfully, and never went picking flowers in the woods.

King of the Cats

(British Isles—England)

On a chilly winter's evening, a gravedigger's wife sat by the fireside, waiting for her husband to come home. Across from her sat her big black cat, Old Tom, who was half asleep, like his mistress.

"Wherever can the man be?" the woman asked.

"Meow," said Old Tom, stretching his legs.

So they waited and waited.

Suddenly both jumped to hear footsteps pounding up the path. A minute later, the gravedigger, all out of breath, came rushing into the room.

"Who's Tom Tildrum?" he shouted in such a wild way that both his wife and his cat stared at him in surprise.

"Why, what's the matter?" asked his wife. "And why do you want to know who Tom Tildrum is?"

The gravedigger caught his breath and pulled a chair up to the fire. "What an adventure I've had! There I was, digging away at old Mr. Fordyce's grave. Hard work it was, so I paused for a rest, sitting in the hole itself, where the wind couldn't reach me. Then I suppose I dropped off to sleep. How long I remained so, I can't say. But I woke up when I heard a cat's *meow.*"

"Meow," said Old Tom in answer.

"Yes, just like that! So I peeped over the edge of the grave, and what do you think I saw?"

"Now, how could I know that?" his wife said. "Get on with the telling."

"Indeed, I saw nine black cats that looked for all the world like our own Tom here," said her husband. "Each had a white spot on its chest, just like him. And what do you think they were carrying?" he asked his wife.

"You might as well ask Old Tom as ask me," said his wife, who was growing impatient, "since we were both of us sitting by the fire."

"Well, those cats were walking upright, and eight of them were carrying a little coffin on their shoulders. It was covered with a black velvet cloth, and the cloth was all bordered in little gold crowns. The ninth cat—bigger than the others—walked in front. At every third step, he would call out, '*Meow!*' Then the others would all answer together, '*Meow!*' "

"*Meow!*" wailed Old Tom again.

"Yes, just like that!" exclaimed the gravedigger. "And as they came nearer and nearer to me, I could see them even more clearly, because their eyes seemed to shine with a strange green light. Well, they all came toward me, and the leader looked for all the world like—but look at our Tom!" the man said, pointing a finger at the cat on the hearth. "See how he's staring at me! You'd think he understood every word I was saying."

"Go on, go on," said his wife. "Never mind Old Tom."

"Well, as I was saying," the gravedigger continued, "those cats came slowly toward me, marching as solemnly as proper mourners, and every third step crying out, '*Meow!*' in answer to the leader's own '*Meow!*' "

"*Meow!*" bawled Old Tom again.

"Yes, just like that," the man said with a nod. "On they came, until they stood alongside Mr. Fordyce's grave. There they stood still and stared right at me. It made me feel odd, that it did! Those nine pair of glowing green eyes peering at me." Then the man looked at his own cat and

said, "But look at Old Tom. He's staring at me just the way they did. And—bless me!—but there seems to be more green in his eyes than I've ever seen before."

"Go on, go on," said his wife, "finish the story and never mind Old Tom!"

"Where was I?" said the man. "Oh, yes, I recall now. Those nine big cats just stood still, looking at me. Then the one that wasn't carrying the coffin came forward, stood on the edge of the grave gazing down at me, and said—"

"Are you saying that the cat *spoke* to you?" his wife asked, shaking her head in disbelief.

Now it was her husband's turn to grow impatient. "*Yes*, I swear to you, he said to me, in a squeaky voice, 'Tell Tom Tildrum that Tim Toldrum is dead.' I was so unnerved, I ran from the churchyard that very minute. And that's why, when I first came in here, I asked you if you know who Tom Tildrum is. How can I tell Tom Tildrum that Tim Toldrum is dead, if I don't for the life of me know who Tom Tildrum is?"

But his wife suddenly shouted, "Look at Old Tom! *Look at Old Tom!*"

Then the both of them gaped, for Old Tom seemed to grow to twice his normal size, while his eyes blazed with a terrible green light. He shrieked out, "What? Old Tim dead? Then *I'm* King of the Cats!"

With a howl of triumph he rushed up the chimney and was nevermore seen by the gravedigger or his wife.

The Dead Mother

(Russia)

Long, long ago, in the days when the czars ruled Russia, a husband and wife lived in a small village. Though they were poor, and their life from day to day was always hard, they remained happy and loving. The mere sight of Ivan and Anya walking hand-in-hand gave pleasure to their neighbors; their shared joy lightened the labors of farmhand and housewife alike.

When the couple found out that they were to have a child, they were delighted. This was the miracle they had been praying for for years. Now their dearest dream would be fulfilled.

But a dark cloud cast its shadow over their happiness. Shortly after Anya bore a son, she died with the infant resting in her arms. To the last, the poor woman's eyes were fixed on the sweet, tiny face of her sleeping child. The sadness and longing in her eyes shattered the already breaking heart of her husband. A moment later, she sighed her last. Then poor Ivan dropped to his knees beside the bed, holding his wife's cold hand, and moaned and wept until his cries woke the child.

Gently he gathered his son into his arms. How was he to bring up his motherless child alone? he wondered. He determined to do the best that he could. So he hired an old woman named Tatiana to look after the baby while he worked in the fields.

But a strange thing happened. All day long the infant would cry endlessly, refusing all food, refusing to be comforted. Yet, during the deepest hours of the night, he remained so quiet that neither Ivan nor old Tatiana sleeping beside the child's cradle was ever disturbed. One might have thought the baby wasn't there at all.

The old woman grew increasingly worried about why a child so fretful by day should remain strangely silent throughout the night. It seemed to her unnatural. Finally, determined to get to the bottom of the mystery, she decided to stay awake and watch until dawn.

The next night, having settled the baby (who had fussed the whole day) as best she could in his cradle, Tatiana sat on the bench near the hearth. By the fire's glow she mended one of Ivan's shirts. From the room behind the curtain she could hear the man's soft snoring.

As the hour grew late, the baby stopped crying. When Tatiana leaned over the cradle to see if he was asleep, she was surprised to find the baby wide-eyed, with a look on his tiny face that suggested he was watching and listening for something. When the infant first saw her, he smiled and stretched his little arms up to her. Then he seemed to recognize her, and screwed up his face as though he would burst into tears. Startled, the old woman stepped back. Instantly the child sighed, and became as quiet and watchful as before.

Puzzled, Tatiana retreated to her corner by the fireplace. She took up her mending, but kept her eyes on the cradle, hardly daring to breathe. An expectant hush had fallen on the room.

Suddenly, just at midnight, she heard someone softly open the door. Looking up, she saw the figure of a woman, shrouded in veils, tiptoe to the cradle. Tatiana tried to call out, but her voice was frozen in her throat as surely as she herself was frozen to the bench.

The stranger's veils were draped over the cradle. From beneath came the sound of the infant's contented gurgling and occasional chuckles of pleasure.

After what seemed like hours, the veiled figure abandoned the cradle and once again tiptoed to the door. When the door was opened, Tatiana could see streaks of dawn light to the east.

The moment the door shut behind the figure, the old woman was able to rise. She ran to the cradle and looked in, but the baby was sleeping peacefully. Yanking the cottage door wide, she gazed across the yard, which was lightly powdered with the first snow of winter. But she saw no trace of the mysterious woman. Not so much as a single footprint marred the smooth expanse of snow.

Uncertain whether she had really seen anything, or had merely fallen asleep beside the fireplace and dreamed it, the old woman decided to say nothing to Ivan. She would keep watch a second night to see what happened.

But the next night, the same thing happened.

When it happened the third night, she told Ivan what she had seen. Deeply troubled, he called together his kinsfolk to ask their advice on what to do.

After much discussion, they decided to stay with Ivan that same night, to see who came to visit the infant in the dead of night. As soon as the sun set, they all lay down on the floor. Ivan rested with them, with a lighted candle hidden beneath an old earthen pot beside his head. The baby, as though troubled by so many people around his cradle, seemed more restless than ever.

At midnight, the door of the cottage slowly opened, just as Tatiana had said. A silken rustling and the sounds of someone tiptoeing toward the cradle could be heard by all. At that instant, the baby ceased his crying and began to gurgle happily. But the watchers felt their limbs growing heavy and their voices catching in their throats. Only Ivan

was able to resist the weariness long enough to reach over and uncover the candle.

In the light, the spell was broken. Ivan scrambled to his feet and held out the taper toward the veiled figure. His eyes grew wide with astonishment and fear when he recognized his beloved Anya, clad in the very same clothes in which she had been buried. She was on her knees beside the cradle, clutching the child to her heart.

Ivan whispered her name as he took a step closer. But the candle suddenly blazed up. At the same instant, she set the infant down in the crib and gazed mournfully at her tiny son. Then she turned and left the room without a sound, with never a word to Ivan or any of his kinsfolk who stood around the chamber, terror-struck.

Ivan stared as the door closed gently behind Anya. Then, with a soft moan, he stooped and picked up the baby. But his moan quickly turned to cries of anguish when he realized that the child he held in his arms was dead.

Knock . . . Knock . . . Knock . . .

(United States/Canada—urban folklore)

You're wearing *that* to a costume party?" exclaimed Nicole. "That's not a *costume*."

"I'm going as a jogger," said Mark.

"You jog every day. That's only your old gray running suit!"

"So, it's authentic," Mark said. "Anyhow, I didn't have time to come up with a real costume."

"You could have rented one," Nicole pointed out.

"I'm not wasting my hard-earned college money on a giant bunny outfit," he said. "Besides, you're dressed up enough for both of us."

"I'm Queen Guinevere," she explained. "You know, she married King Arthur."

"Yeah, I saw the movie on TV," Mark said. "Um, Nic. Just to put you on yellow alert, my car's been giving me a little trouble."

Nicole sighed. "Will it get us there?"

"Ninety-eight percent certainty."

"And back?" she wondered, then added quickly, "Don't give me the odds: Just get us there. We'll work the rest out later."

"You got it!" Mark said, offering her his arm. "Queen Guinevere, your Toyota awaits."

"Lancelot you're not," she said, laughing. "But you do look pretty good—even in a grungy jogging suit."

.   .   .

However, Nicole's high spirits soon evaporated. Mark's car managed nearly to stall out at every stop sign or intersection.

"Are you sure we'll get to the country club?" she asked anxiously.

"Yeah, I'm sure," Mark snapped as the engine sputtered and the car shuddered.

Nicole held her breath, but the problem seemed to correct itself. It wasn't just the car that made her jittery; a heavy fog had settled over the lonely, twisting country road.

"Relax, put on some music," Mark suggested, adding quickly, "—um, on the radio. The cassette player is broken."

Nicole almost said something about what bad shape everything was in, but she decided not to risk an argument. As the hills grew higher, the music stations faded into static. All she could get was a news station.

"Great," she said, making a face. Then she paused, listening intently, as the radio announced:

". . . warning everyone in the Norris Valley area that convicted killer Owen Helms—the so-called Hangman—has escaped from the criminal asylum at Pinecrest . . ."

"That's just at the other end of the valley!" cried Nicole. She was going to *insist* that Mark turn the car around, when two things happened. The radio program dissolved into crackling static, and the car bucked twice and died. Mark used what momentum was left to steer the Toyota to the side of the road. They came to a stop under a tree. Condensed fog dripped from an overhanging branch, *thunk, thunk, thunk.*

Mark turned the ignition key several times, but all the engine would do was gurgle and chuff. Soon even these noises grew weaker. The car refused to start.

Finally Nicole said, "Give it a rest; you're just draining the battery."

Mark slammed his fist against the steering wheel. Then he climbed out, lifted the hood, and fiddled with the engine.

"Try it now!" he'd call every few minutes. But when Nicole turned the key, all she got were clicks. In between, she tried to get some more news on the escaped killer. But the radio just gave off creepy sounds like whispers, so she snapped it off.

"I'm going to have to go and get help. Lucky I wore my jog togs and Nikes after all. I think we're just a few miles from the country club. I'll call a tow truck from there, then have someone bring me back here. I shouldn't be gone more than a half hour or so."

"No way am I staying out here by myself," said Nicole. "Not with the Happy Hangman on the loose."

"Be reasonable, Nic! How are you gonna jog in that costume of yours? And I'm not about to go for a stroll through this freezing fog."

"No, Mark, *please!*"

"If you're really worried, crouch down on the floor in back under the old blanket. If anyone comes along, they'll think the car is empty. But no one will bother you, I promise."

"You also promised to get us to the party," she said. But she was more scared than angry. "Oh, all right—but I *swear* I'm not coming out from under that blanket until I'm sure it's you."

"I'm gonna leave you the keys for safekeeping. When I get back, I'll knock three times, like this." He went *knock . . . knock . . . knock . . .* on the roof of the car, just above the door on the driver's side. "Don't come out until you hear that signal."

"I won't," she said, "believe me."

He kissed her good-bye, watched while she locked and tested both doors, then waved as he jogged away into the fog. The minute he was out of sight, she climbed into the backseat, bunched up in the narrow space, and arranged the musty old blanket over herself.

How long she remained there Nicole wasn't sure. When her legs began to cramp, she brought her watch up to her face without disturbing the blanket and read the illuminated dial. Less than half an hour had passed, but it felt more like years.

Suddenly she heard a *knock* on the roof of the car.

"Mark," she whispered. She was about to throw off the blanket, when she remembered he'd promised to knock *three* times. She had a sudden, sickening feeling that someone else was outside—maybe trying to find a way into the locked car.

"Please, please, knock again," she whispered. "Make it be Mark!"

Knock.

"Once more—please; just once more."

Knock.

She almost laughed out loud with relief . . .

Knock.

Her blood turned to ice water.

Knock . . . knock . . . knock . . .

She froze, hardly daring to breathe, as the knocks continued on and on, spaced just about the same. Each one was like a fist in her stomach.

At first she was sure that the Hangman was trying to get in. Then she imagined that he was so wacko that he was just beating on the car like a child pounding endlessly on a toy drum. Finally she wondered if he *knew* she was inside, and was tormenting her until he smashed a window.

Knock . . . knock . . . knock . . .

"Please, someone, come help me!" she prayed.

Knock . . . knock . . .

Then she heard the sound of heavy boots crunching on the gravel. Voices. And a radio, with a dispatcher's voice giving instructions that she couldn't make out.

Knock.

Then, mercifully, it stopped. Mark must have come. Or the tow truck. Nicole sat up and looked out the window— and screamed!

Two men were staring in at her. After a terrifying, confused moment, she realized that they were police. Behind them she saw the spinning blue and red lights on top of their police car.

"It's okay, young lady," the first officer said. "You can come out now."

Her shaking hand found the lock release. She climbed unsteadily out.

"Where's Mark?" she asked, looking around. "Didn't he come with you?"

"Come to the patrol car," said the second officer. "*Don't look back*—just keep your eyes on the patrol car."

"Why can't I look?" Nicole asked. She turned suddenly and saw Mark's body, still in the gray jogging outfit, hanging from the tree limb above the car.

"Hey!" yelled the officer. "You don't want to see this, miss!" As he reached out to grab her the body started swinging. Nicole watched in horror as one Nike-clad foot began to beat against the roof of the car:

Knock . . . knock . . . knock . . .

Twice Surprised

(Japan)

Late one winter night, a schoolteacher was walking along a road that ran beside a rice field. To his surprise, he discovered a lovely young woman seated on a large, white stone at the edge of the field. Her face was hidden from him as she read, by moonlight, a book spread open on her lap.

Surprised to find anyone else on the lonely road so late, the man greeted her politely. She nodded, but did not look up from her book.

"What text are you studying so carefully?" he asked.

Still, she did not answer him or look up.

Finally the teacher said lightly, "Is it wise for you to be alone out here so late at night? This is the hour when ghosts are prowling about, you know. Perhaps I am a ghost myself."

She did not respond to his little joke, but she looked up at him. The top half of her face was a mass of ghastly, glittering eyes all different sizes and colors. The lower half of her face split wide open from side to side, revealing a serpent's jaws with bared fangs. From deep within her throat came a warning growl.

One look at her horrible face, and the teacher fled in terror, his coat thrown over his head for fear he might see that ghastly face again.

The unfortunate man was gasping for breath and still trembling when he reached his home. Though the house

was quite warm, he felt as cold as if he were lost in the heart of a blizzard.

His wife, without looking up from the letter she was writing, asked him, "Why are you so out of breath and distressed?"

"I saw something horrible on my way home," her husband answered. "It must have been a ghost or a demon."

"What did it look like?" she asked.

"It appeared, in the moonlight, to be a beautiful young woman," he said.

"If she was beautiful," his wife asked, her inkbrush gracefully shaping characters on the page in front of her, "why were you frightened?"

"When she looked up at me, her face was horrible! *Horrible!*" said the man, beginning to shake again.

"What did it look like?" his wife asked.

"I cannot describe it," the poor man said, "it was so terrible. One cannot capture in words how frightful that face was."

"But what did it look like?" his wife persisted.

"I cannot tell you what it looked like," the teacher answered helplessly.

"Was it this kind of face?" his wife asked. So saying, she turned away from her letter, toward her husband. Before him was the horrible face he had seen in the moonlight. But now it seemed to grow until it filled the room with dreadful eyes and teeth.

Scared out of his wits, the man gave a cry of terror, then sank senseless to the floor.

When he awoke the next morning, the sun was shining brightly on him as he lay facedown beside a large white stone at the edge of the road.

Notes on Sources

"HOLD HIM, TABB!" This African-American ghost story from Virginia was originally published in the *Southern Workman and Hampton School Record* (Vol. 26, No. 6, June 1897, Hampton, Va.: Hampton Normal & Agricultural Institute). It was reprinted in the *Journal of American Folk-Lore* and in B. A. Botkin's *A Treasury of Southern Folklore: Stories, Ballads, Traditions, and Folkways of the People of the South* (New York: Crown Publishers, 1949). I have closely followed the original narrative, adding only some details and dialogue.

THE WITCHES' EYES. I have retold this story, familiar throughout the southwestern United States and Mexico, from many variant readings, including versions in José Manuel Espinosa's *Spanish Folk-Tales from New Mexico* (Memoirs of the American Folk-Lore Society, Vol. XXX, 1937, New York: Kraus Reprint Company, 1976), Riley Aiken's *Mexican Tales from the Borderland: From the Publications of the Texas Folklore Society* (Dallas: Southern Methodist University Press, 1980), and John O. West's *Mexican-American Folklore: Legends, Songs, Festivals, Proverbs, Crafts, Tales of Saints, of Revolutionaries, and More* (Little Rock: August House, Inc., 1988). Additional details came from numerous sources, including Aurora Lucero-White Lea's *Literary Folklore of the Hispanic Southwest* (San Antonio, Tex.: The Naylor Company, 1953).

THE DUPPY. This original tale incorporates Caribbean folklore from a variety of sources, including Zora Neale Hurston's groundbreaking study of Haitian folklore, *Tell My Horse* (New York: Lippincott & Crowell Publishers, 1938; reprint, New York: HarperCollins, 1989). See also the excellent article "Parallels in West African, West Indian, and North Carolina Folklore" in *North Carolina Folklore* (Vol. XVII, No. 2, November 1969, Raleigh: North Carolina Folklore Society) by David K. Evans, Don Stephen Rice, and Joanne Kline Partin. They note that "duppy" may come from "doorpeep," suggesting something peeping through a keyhole, or from the West African Ashanti *dupon*, referring to the thick roots of certain trees in which duppies may live. In Sierra Leone in West Africa, the word refers to ancestors who watch over villages. In Jamaica it can mean a ghost or other supernatural being. See also *Funk & Wagnalls Standard Dictionary of Folklore, Mythology, and Legend: An Unabridged*

Edition of the Original Work with a Key to Place Names, Cultures, and People, edited by Maria Leach (New York: Harper & Row, Publishers, Inc., 1949, 1950, 1972; paperback reprint, Harper San Francisco, 1982).

TWO SNAKES. Retold from a tale that appears under the title "Two Snakes" in *100 Chinese Myths and Fantasies,* selected and translated by Ding Wangdao (Beijing: Foreign Language Teaching and Research Press; published and printed in Hong Kong, n.d.). The same tale, under the title "The Hunter," appears in *The Man Who Sold a Ghost: Chinese Tales of the 3rd–6th Centuries,* translated by Yang Hsien-Yi and Gladys Yang (Hong Kong: The Commercial Press, 1958, 1977).

THE DRAUG. Retold from various accounts in *Phantoms and Fairies from Norwegian Folklore,* Tor Age Bringsvaerd, translated by Pat Shaw Iversen (Oslo, Norway: Johan Grundt Tanum Forlag, n.d.). Published in cooperation with the Department of Cultural Relations, Ministry of Foreign Affairs. Other accounts are found in Reider Christiansen's *Folktales of Norway* (Chicago: The University of Chicago Press, 1964). Christiansen comments, "The *Draug* . . . is a sinister, malevolent being, and his appearance is an omen of impending disaster. In the tradition his name is identical with Old Norse *draugr,* i.e., ghost, or more precisely, 'a living dead person.' "

THE VAMPIRE CAT. Retold from an account in A. B. Mitford (Lord Redesdale), *Tales of Old Japan* (first published in London in 1871; reprinted, Boston: Charles E. Tuttle, 1966). The tale is also available in many other collections. Additional details were incorporated from Lafcadio Hearn, *Kwaidan: Stories and Studies of Strange Things* (Boston: Houghton, Mifflin, and Company, 1904; reprinted, Boston: Charles E. Tuttle Company, 1971).

WINDIGO ISLAND. This story is a prose retelling, somewhat amplified, of a poem by William Henry Drummond (1854–1907), "The Windigo," originally published in *Johnny Corteau and Other Poems* (1901), and reprinted in *Windigo: An Anthology of Fact and Fantastic Fiction,* edited by John Robert Colombo (Saskatoon, Sask.: Western Prairie Books, 1982; distributed by The University of Nebraska Press). I incorporated details from E. W. Thomson's "Red-Headed Windego" (1895), also reprinted in the Colombo anthology. The lyrics to *"En Roulant Ma Boule"* ("A-rolling My Bowl") come from the chapter titled "Songs of the Voyageurs" in *Were-Wolves and Will-o-the-Wisps: French Tales of Mackinac Retold,* written and illustrated by Dirk Gringhuis (Mackinac Island, Mich.: Mackinac Island State Park Commission, 1974). Additional information and gruesomely fascinating accounts can be found in *Where the Chill Came From: Cree Windigo Tales and Journeys,* gathered and translated by Howard Norman (San Francisco: North Point Press, 1982).

THE HAUNTED INN. This story from classical China has been retold in many versions. Readers might want to consult Bernhardt J Hurwood's *Passport to the Supernatural* (New York: Taplinger Publishing Company, 1972) and Bernhardt J. Hurwood's *Monsters Galore* (New York: Fawcett Publications, 1965), or

Classical Chinese Tales of the Supernatural and Fantastic: Selections from the Third to the Tenth Century, edited by Karl S. Y. Kao (Bloomington: Indiana University Press, 1985).

THE ROLLING HEAD. I based this tale on accounts by plains people, enhancing the descriptions of Hungry Old Woman and Snake Old Man from parallel texts. Key sources include a Blackfeet account in Lewis Spence, *North American Indians: Myths and Legends* (London: George G. Harrap & Company, 1914; reprinted, London: Bracken Books, 1986) and a Cheyenne narrative in *Indian Tales of North America: An Anthology for the Adult Reader,* edited by Tristram P. Coffin (Philadelphia: American Folklore Society, 1961).

Coffin notes that "the motif of the rolling head is worldwide, being known to Europeans, Indonesians, and Africans, as well as to the North American Indians." The Cheyenne version has the young girl use quills and a root digger to escape the head and save her brother. The Blackfeet tale has two boys use a stick, a stone, and water squeezed from moss. The Modocs of northern California and southern Oregon tell of a monstrous, man-eating head that is disposed of by two old women, who promise to ferry the head across a stream, but push it into the water instead (Jeremiah Curtain, *Myths of the Modocs,* published in 1912; reissued, New York: Benjamin Blom, 1971).

THE CROGLIN GRANGE VAMPIRE. This account first appeared in a book called *In My Solitary Life* by Augustus Hare (4 volumes; London: Allen, 1896–1901), and has been reprinted in *Aidan Chambers' Book of Ghosts and Hauntings* (originally published, London: Longman Young Books, 1973; reissued, Hammondsworth, England: Kestrel Books/Penguin Books, 1981); Raymond T. McNally, *A Clutch of Vampires* (New York: Bell Publishing Company, 1974); and, somewhat recast, in Nancy Garden, *Vampires* (New York: J. B. Lippincott Company, 1973). Charles Harper, in his book *Haunted Houses* (1924), said there was no place called Croglin Grange. Others pointed out that part of Hare's report resembled the novel *Varney the Vampire* (London: 1847).

But in the Spring 1963 issue of *Tomorrow* magazine, F. Clive Ross claimed he visited the area in Britain where the events Hare reported took place. Ross said he met a woman who had known a Mr. Fisher, a member of the family that, according to the story, owned Croglin Grange. Born in the 1860s, Mr. Fisher said he had heard the tale from his grandparents who told him these events happened between 1680 and 1690, rather than 1875, as Hare reported.

THE YARA. This legend is adapted from "The Yara," by Brazilian journalist and historian Affonso Arinhos de Melo Franco (1868–1916), reprinted in *The Golden Land: An Anthology of Latin American Folklore in Literature,* selected, edited, and translated by Harriet de Onis (New York: Alfred A. Knopf, 1948); and from Frances Carpenter, "Mario and the Yara," *South American Wonder Tales* (Chicago and New York: Follett Publishing Company, 1969). Details of Indian life and culture, as well as natural history, came from such sources as Alex Shoumatoff, *The Rivers Amazon* (San Francisco: Sierra Club Books, 1978, revised 1986), and F. Bruce Lamb, *Wizard of the Upper Amazon: The Story of Manuel Cordova-Rios* (Boston: Houghton Mifflin Company, 1971, revised 1974).

Affonso Arinhos de Melo Franco calls the people "the Manaus," but it is unclear whether that names a tribe or merely a village. He might refer to ancestors of the reclusive Waimiri-Atroari tribe, whom Alex Shoumatoff describes in 1978 as living in nine villages 150 miles north of the present-day town of Manaus.

"ME, MYSELF". Adapted from J. F. Campbell, *Popular Tales of the West Highlands, Orally Collected: New Edition* (London: Alexander Gardner Publisher, 1890). Campbell notes that this "is a story which is all over the [Scottish] Highlands in various shapes."

Added facts about the Hebrides Islands come from John McPhee, *The Crofter & the Laird* (New York: Farrar, Straus & Giroux, 1969), which explains: "The large seeds of a treelike West Indian plant called *Entada scandens* have drifted to the shores of [the islands] for thousands of years, and they have always been called fairy eggs. People once wore them around their necks, believing that this protected them from the evil moods of fairies." Other references include Ronald Macdonald Douglas, *Scottish Lore and Folklore* (New York: Beekman House, 1982), and Lillian Beckwith, *The Hills Is Lonely* (New York: E. P. Dutton & Company, 1963), an account of the author's stay in the Hebrides.

ISLAND OF FEAR. Retold from "The Island of the Cannibal" in Arthur C. Parker, *Seneca Myths & Folk Tales* (originally published, Buffalo, New York: Buffalo Historical Society, 1923; reissued, Lincoln: University of Nebraska/ Bison Books, 1989), and "The Friendly Skeleton" in Lewis Spence, *North American Indians: Myths & Legends* (original publication: London: George G. Harrap & Company, 1914; reprinted, London: Bracken Books, 1985). Many other versions have been recorded from Native American storytellers throughout the Northeast region.

THREE WHO SOUGHT DEATH. Adapted from "The Pardoner's Tale" in Geoffrey Chaucer's *The Canterbury Tales,* from *The Works of Geoffrey Chaucer,* edited by F. N. Robinson, second edition (Boston: Houghton Mifflin Company, 1933, 1957). Versions of this moral tale turn up in the literature of ancient India, Arabia, Italy, and central Asia.

SISTER DEATH AND THE HEALER. This widely known Hispanic tale from the Mexican-American border region is rooted in an older story from Spain. Among many versions consulted were those in John O. West, *Mexican-American Folklore: Legends, Songs, Festivals, Proverbs, Crafts, Tales of Saints, of Revolutionaries, and More* (Little Rock: August House, 1988); José Griego y Maestas and Rudolfo A. Anaya, *Cuentos: Tales from the Hispanic Southwest: Bilingual Stories in Spanish and English* (Santa Fe: Museum of New Mexico Press, 1980); and the Editors of Time-Life Books, *The Enchanted World: Tales of Terror* (Chicago:

Time-Life Books, 1987). For my retelling, I borrowed a few details from Spanish counterparts.

THE MOUSE TOWER. Adapted from accounts in *Curious Myths of the Middle Ages* by Reverend Sabine Baring-Gould (London: Rivingtons, 1866), and an account in *The German Legends of the Brothers Grimm, Volume I,* edited and translated by Donald Ward (Philadelphia, Penn.: Institute for the Study of Human Issues Incorporated, 1981). The Grimms' work was originally published in 1816. See also *The Finest Legends of the Rhine* by Wilhelm Ruland (Bonn, Germany: Stollfuss Verlag, 1969).

Baring-Gould argues that the real-life Bishop Hatto was not "hard-hearted and wicked" and that "the [mouse] tower was erected as a station for collecting tolls on vessels passing up and down the river." Maria Leach, editor of *Funk & Wagnalls Standard Dictionary of Folklore, Mythology, and Legend,* notes that stories of a miser devoured by mice or rats in a tower are widespread throughout Germany, Austria, Switzerland, Poland, and Scandinavia.

THE DEVIL AND TOM WALKER. This account was first published in Washington Irving, *Tales of a Traveller* (New York: 1825; reprinted in *The Works of Washington Irving, Volume I,* New York: P. F. Collier, n.d.). Folklorist Richard M. Dorson, in his *Jonathan Draws the Long Bow: New England Popular Tales and Legends* (Cambridge, Mass.: Harvard University Press, 1946), comments that it is a literary tale that has evolved into regional folklore, noting that the story was included in Charles M. Skinner's *Myths and Legends of Our Own Land, Volume I* (Philadelphia: J. B. Lippincott Company, 1896).

I have omitted many of Irving's satirical jabs at business, politics, and social custom, and the subtext about Tom Walker's wife. But the text remains substantially Irving's, with only minimal additions for the sake of continuity or clarity.

THE GREEDY DAUGHTER. Adapted from the story of the same title originally published in R. H. Busk, *The Folk-Lore of Rome* (n.d.), reprinted in *Folk Tales of All Nations,* edited by F. H. Lee (New York: Tudor Publishing Company, 1930). I also consulted the more extended and earthier version titled "Uncle Wolf" in *Italian Folktales,* selected and retold by Italo Calvino, published in Italy in 1956; English translation by George Martin (New York: Harcourt Brace Jovanovich, 1980); available in paperback in *The Pantheon Fairy Tale and Folklore Library* (New York: Random House, 1981).

THE PIRATE. Adapted from Richard H. Dana's eighteenth-century poem "The Buccaneer," reprinted with commentary in Samuel Adams Drake, *A Book of New England Legends and Folk Lore: In Prose and Poetry* (first edition, 1884; revised, 1906; reprinted, Boston: Charles E. Tuttle, 1971). I have also consulted the prose version by Charles M. Skinner in his *Myths and Legends of Our Own Land* (Philadelphia: J. B. Lippincott Company, 1896). These accounts are loosely based on the actual burning of the ship *Palantine* in the winter of 1750–51, which gave rise to many tales about a blazing ghostly vessel.

THE GOLDEN ARM. Adapted and expanded from Joseph Jacobs, *English Fairy Tales* (London, 1890), this tale is akin to such formula stories as the English "Teeny Tiny," in which a teeny-tiny woman takes a teeny-tiny bone from a churchyard to make some teeny-tiny soup, and "Tailypo," from the American South, retold in the first volume of *Short & Shivery* (New York: Bantam Doubleday Dell, 1986).

Folklorist Maria Leach comments in her *The Thing at the Foot of the Bed: And Other Scary Tales* (Cleveland, Ohio: William Collins & World Publishing Company, 1959; reprinted by New York: Bantam Doubleday Dell, 1977), "This is one of the most famous scary stories told. It is said to have been told around every Boy and Girl Scout campfire ever kindled . . . the story Mark Twain used to tell to scare whole audiences."

THE SERPENT WOMAN. This tale has been condensed and rewritten from the story of the same title originally published in Mrs. Middlemore, *Spanish Legendary Tales* (n.d.), reprinted in *Folk Tales of All Nations* edited by F. H. Lee (New York: Tudor Publishing Company, 1930). The story uses the familiar element of the witch transformed into another form (black cat, raven, serpent) and discovered when a wound inflicted on the animal is revealed in its human form. For a parallel, one might look at "The Witch Cat" in my first *Short & Shivery* collection.

There is also an echo of the swan-maiden or seal-maiden motif in which magical beings put aside a coat of feathers or a fishskin to become beautiful, seemingly human women.

LOFT THE ENCHANTER. Adapted from accounts in *Ghosts, Witchcraft, and the Other World: Icelandic Folktales I,* translated by Alan Boucher (Reykjavik, Iceland: Iceland Review Library, 1977) and *Legends of Icelandic Magicians,* translated by Jacqueline Simpson (Cambridge, England: D. S. Brewer, Ltd.; Totowa, N.J.: Rowan and Littlefield, 1975). Additional background details are from *Nagel's Encyclopedia-Guide: Iceland, Third Edition, Completely Revised* (Geneva, Paris, Munich: Nagel Publishers, 1984), and *A Family in Iceland: Families Around the World Series* (New York: The Bookwright Press, 1985).

THE ACCURSED HOUSE. Adapted and expanded from an account in Charles M. Skinner, *Myths & Legends of Our Own Land: Volume II* (Philadelphia: J. B. Lippincott Company, 1896). This story picks up the classic folkloric theme of the ghost who guards a hidden treasure.

ESCAPE UP THE TREE. I based this story on a Nigerian version of a well-known African tale because of the unique form the pursuing creature takes. I have added details from Caribbean versions—clearly from African roots— from the islands of Trinidad, Martinique, Dominica, Guadeloupe, Les Saintes, and Haiti. In these stories, a witch, a female demon, or the devil himself forces a boy/young man to escape up the tree. The tale has similarities to "Brother and Sister" in the first *Short & Shivery* collection. In the United States, a variant story is widely known as "Wiley and the Hairy Man." Here a young boy is eventually trapped by the hairy man or the devil, and is rescued by his three (or four) dogs.

For the originals, see "The Hunter and the Witch" in *Nigerian Folk Tales,* as told by Olawale Idewu and Omotayo Adu (New Brunswick, N.J.: Rutgers University Press, 1961). See also variants grouped under the heading "Escape up the Tree" in *Folk-Lore of the Antilles, French and English, Part III,* by Elsie Clews Parsons (first published by the American Folk-Lore Society in 1943; reprinted, New York: Kraus Reprint Company, 1969). Maria Leach discusses the tale in *God Had a Dog: Folklore of the Dog* (New Brunswick, N.J.: Rutgers University Press, 1961).

THE HEADREST. Retold from Annie Ker's *Papuan Fairy Tales* (c. 1912), a collection of folktales from the northeastern coast of New Guinea, reprinted in F. H. Lee, *Folk Tales of All Nations* (New York: Tudor Publishing Company, 1930). Mrs. Ker lived at a mission compound in New Guinea in 1910.

THE THING IN THE WOODS. Adapted from an account in *Gumbo Ya-Ya: A Collection of Louisiana Folk Tales* by Lyle Saxon, Robert Tallant, and Edward Dryer (first published in 1945 by Louisiana Writers Project Publications; reprinted, New York: Bonanza Books, n.d.). Details of Cajun life and language came from William Faulkner Rushton, *The Cajuns: From Acadia to Louisiana* (New York: Farrar, Straus & Giroux, 1970), and other sources.

The Cajuns live mainly in rural southern Louisiana, are largely Roman Catholic, and are the largest French-speaking group in the United States. "Cajun" comes from "Acadian," referring to the part of Canada to which their ancestors came from France. Those early French settlers immigrated to Louisiana after their farms were seized and burned by the English governor of Nova Scotia in 1755. Henry Wadsworth Longfellow tells the story of their exile in his poem *Evangeline.*

KING OF THE CATS. Adapted from Joseph Jacobs's classic *More English Fairy Tales* (London, 1894). Jacobs's version, which is widely anthologized, was put together by that author from several earlier narratives. He cites five variants of the legend, commenting, "An interesting example of the spread and development of a single anecdote throughout England . . . a tale which is, in its way, as weird and fantastic as E[dgar] A[llan] Poe."

THE DEAD MOTHER. Retold from *Russian Folk Tales* by William R. Shedden-Ralston (London, 1873); reprinted in Bernhardt J. Hurwood, *Passport to the Supernatural: An Occult Compendium from All Ages and Many Lands* (New York: Taplinger Publishing Company, 1972).

KNOCK . . . KNOCK . . . KNOCK . . . A retelling of one of the most popular examples of urban folklore. In *The Vanishing Hitchhiker: American Urban Legends & Their Meanings* (New York: W. W. Norton & Company, 1981), Jan Harold Brunvand offers an extended discussion of this "well-known urban legend that folklorists have named 'The Boyfriend's Death' . . . a story that has traveled rapidly to reach nationwide oral circulation." In *Folklore of Can-*

ada (Canada: McClelland and Stewart, 1976), Edith Fowke refers to "The Boyfriend's Death" as being "widely known today. . . . Such legends are particularly rife among teen-agers, who sometimes call them 'scary stories.' These tales, which are always sworn to be true, are told at social get-togethers such as pajama parties, nights at summer camps, canoe trips, or camp reunions."

TWICE SURPRISED. This is one of the most widely repeated ghost stories in Japan. It is known variously under such titles as "Surprised Twice," "The Terrible Face," "The Ghost Covered with Eyes," "The Face That Grew Long," "The Eyeless Demon in Monjuroku," and "Was It This Kind of Face?"

I have based this retelling on a version in *Ancient Tales in Modern Japan: An Anthology of Japanese Folk Tales,* selected and translated by Fanny Hagin Mayer (Bloomington: Indiana University Press, copublished with *Asian Folklore Studies,* 1984), and on a study of the story and its variants found in *The Yanagita Kunio Guide to the Japanese Folk Tale* by Yanagita Kunio, translated and edited by Fanny Hagin Mayer (Bloomington: Indiana University Press, copublished with *Asian Folklore Studies,* 1986). The latter volume is a translation of *Nihon Mukashibanashi Meii,* originally published in Tokyo in 1948.

About the Author

Robert D. San Souci is the award-winning author of many books for young readers, including *Larger Than Life, Young Merlin, Young Guinevere, Feathertop, The Legend of Sleepy Hollow, Sootface,* and *The Hobyahs.* Widely traveled and a popular speaker, he has lectured in schools, libraries, universities, and conferences in more than thirty states. A native Californian, Robert San Souci lives in the San Francisco Bay Area.